The fight was over. No more mortars fell on the meadow where the unit was cleaning up. The CH-13 chopper came sweeping back to take care of any Yugoslavian militia stragglers, but by the time it reached the open ground, none of the unfriendlies were alive. The Leathernecks had seen to that.

Once the mortar pit was blown, the Marines had broken from cover. They had killed two of the enemy who fired back, but several more got up and waved their hands in the air. They were shot anyway. In the grunts' minds, they had perpetrated too much horror to be left alive.

The Yugos fell to the ground with stunned expressions on their faces. After terrorizing the countryside for so long, they had never figured the Americans could be as utterly ruthless as they themselves were. It became their final lesson in life. Americans were not soft. It was the last thing they learned before a burst of 5.56 millimeter shells blew them straight to hell . . .

*Titles by David Alexander*

**MARINE FORCE ONE**
**SPECIAL OPS**
**SHADOW DOWN**

# MARINE FORCE ONE

## David Alexander

BERKLEY BOOKS, NEW YORK

This is a work of fiction. Names, characters, places, and incidents are
either the product of the author's imagination or are used fictitiously,
and any resemblance to actual persons, living or dead, business
establishments, events, or locales is entirely coincidental.

## MARINE FORCE ONE

A Berkley Book / published by arrangement with
the author

PRINTING HISTORY
Berkley edition / September 2001

All rights reserved.
Copyright © 2001 by David Alexander.

This book, or parts thereof, may not be reproduced in
any form without permission.
For information address: The Berkley Publishing Group,
a division of Penguin Putnam Inc.,
375 Hudson Street, New York, New York 10014.

Readers can E-mail the author at
www.feedback@davidalexanderbooks.com

Visit our website at
www.penguinputnam.com

ISBN: 0-425-18152-9

BERKLEY®
Berkley Books are published by The Berkley Publishing Group,
a division of Penguin Putnam Inc.,
375 Hudson Street, New York, New York 10014.
BERKLEY and the "B" design
are trademarks belonging to Penguin Putnam Inc.

PRINTED IN THE UNITED STATES OF AMERICA

10  9  8  7  6  5  4  3  2  1

"We've got the nerve."
—Marine Corps saying

book one **Snake Eyes**

# chapter *one*

The V-22 Osprey lifted vertically from the flight deck of the USS *Eisenhower*, a Nimitz class nuclear carrier standing off the Adriatic coast of southern Albania. At the Osprey's 60-foot translation altitude, the convertiplane's mammoth tilt-rotor engine nacelles pivoted forward to engage in horizontal flight mode. Now flying levelly at twice the speed of any chopper in anybody else's military, the V-22 ferried the Marine specwar detachment known as Cobra Force inland on a back-door recon. Like other covert missions conducted by the team, this too was to be a recon by fire.

Inside the V-22's passenger and cargo bay, the Marine they called Chicken Wire gave the two

FNGs seated on the opposite bulkhead his best gimlet-eyed once-over. Damn, but they sure looked green.

The FNGs—fucking new guys—were to take the place of two Cobra Force team members killed in action on the elite special operations detachment's prior mission into Bosnia some weeks back. All these FNGs knew about war they'd learned from combat simulations, training excercises, crap like that, C.W. surmised. Still, they'd aced out dozens of other candidates who would have given their right nut to be part of the team.

Chicken Wire figured they'd do okay—nobody was just seconded into the unit. You had to prove yourself worthy. More importantly, Major David Saxon, the unit commander, had to give the green light first, and Saxon was not an easy dude to bullshit.

Still, he wondered, do I want to trust my ass with these greenhorns?

Well, screw it. The fact was that C.W. trusted nobody but C.W. and Pauline, his true-blue Pig. C.W. kept Pauline, an M60E3 Maremont machine gun, tuned up like a Stradivarius violin. With a couple hundred rounds of NATO standard in Pauline's box mag, there wasn't any number C.W. couldn't play.

Chicken Wire was the team's squad auto weapon gunner, the SAW-man or the Pig Meister, depending on who you talked to. Most guys in the unit had a nickname, and like many another jarhead in the detachment, Chicken Wire didn't have a clue as to where his own had come from. He'd just been tagged with the handle one fine day during his basic at Camp Lejeune and had worn it ever since.

Not that he really had cause for complaint. Chicken Wire once knew a Marine they'd called Crazy Gonorrhea Face. He also knew a seven-foot black guy with muscles in his shit they called Pussy, but never to his face. Getting tired of staring at the FNGs, Chicken Wire leaned forward. He had a question for them.

"Yo—either of you know a guy named Pussy?" he asked.

C.W. smiled, waiting for one of them to answer.

Cobra Force's official designation was MF-1, Marine Force One, a special operations detachment of the 1st Marine Expeditionary Unit (MEU). It was trained in small unit warfare, counterterrorist ops— in fact, counter-anything-you-got operations. Unofficially, the unit was called Cobra Force by its members and by practically everyone else.

Anything the Navy SEALs or the Army Delta Force did, the fighting leathernecks of Cobra Force did better, faster and smarter. What the hell, they were Marines, weren't they?

Cobra's mission was to deal with a problem that had been giving Marine tacair some major headaches lately over the craggy, tree-studded ridge lines and thickly forested valleys of southeastern Montenegro. The Serb regional missile commander known as Count Dracula was a hammered-down, tough-as-nails, shit-dipped sonofabitch who had been making things pretty rough for F/A-18 strike packages inbound for targets on the Macedonia-Bulgaria borders and the mission planners at EUCOM; he'd been up to his shenanigans for weeks. The air arm of the carrier battle group loitering off the coast of Albania had suffered unacceptable losses during the two week old Operation Eastern Star.

This was no small accomplishment. But all good things must come to an end, including Count Dracula's winning streak against NATO. The renegade Serb now lived on borrowed time. A cobra was fixing to bite him on the ass.

The president had made a special webcast from the White House to address the nation on what was happening and why the United States was committing ground troops to a foreign civil war for the first time since the Gulf War. His address put it in terms similar to George Bush's explanation fifteen years before: oil and jobs. And one more thing: the threat of global nuclear annihilation.

The resurgent Soviet Union had expanded into Bulgaria, and the Bulgarians had intruded into Macedonia. At stake were the strategic oil fields of the Black and Caspian Seas. These fields weren't that important to the United States, explained the president, but they were important enough to the European Economic Community for the EEC to risk unilateral action—even if that meant baiting the Russian Bear on its home turf. If ESDI, the European Self-Defense Initiative combat force, struck out unilaterally, it could turn a limited regional war into a global conflict, and possibly lead to nuclear escalation.

The United States had only one recourse if it was to prevent this potential powder keg from erupting, and that was to use its high-technology weapons to roll back the Soviets and their Bulgarian allies before the neo-communist bloc swallowed up Macedonia, Montenegro and the rest of the Balkans.

After that the U.N. could step in and sort out the assholes from the harp players. This meant, however, that U.S. ground troops would be committed to the war. Such was the rationale behind Eastern Star.

The operation got off to a bad start, though, and Count Dracula was the main reason. When it commenced, the air war's first objective was to neutralize the SAM belt girding the southwestern approach to the Yugoslavian interior. The surface-to-air missile belt stretched in a broken line along a north-south axis, from its origins in the mountainous hinterlands to within a few kilometers of the Greek frontier.

CIA analysts had spent considerable time and taxpayers' money studying overhead imagery of the SAM belt from an Improved Crystal photointelligence satellite and from SR-71 Blackbird overflights in the weeks prior to the mission's launch. The intel take showed the belt was made up mostly of mobile SAM TELs—transporter-erector-launchers—with a small scattering of fixed sites mixed in among them.

Some of the SAMs were old SA-8s, which could be bypassed by flying in attack sorties at high altitudes, but many others were recent versions of SA-10s that couldn't be reliably dealt with by electronic countermeasures and high-envelope overflight tactics. Those SAMs had the range and navigational systems to home in on even air-dominance combat aircraft with lethal effectiveness.

This meant that the SAMs could not just simply be bypassed but had to be taken out, reduced to slag. The Navy felt it had just the thing to do the job. In addition to the Tomahawk Land Attack Missile (TLAM), the Navy had begun fielding the upgraded SLAM-ER (Standoff Land Attack Missile Expanded Response) missile just before the hostilities began. Both cruise missiles were accurate and deadly stand-off munitions.

In the predawn hours the fleet began launching in-bound TLAMs and SLAM-ERs at SAM installations in the Macedonian belt. At first light, the Improved Crystal orbital imagery and Blackbird spy plane missions brought in new pictures from which battle damage assessments were compiled by the intel staff at EUCOM. By midday more missiles were again inbound.

After three consecutive days of standoff attack, the SAM force was decimated. But decimated was not the same as destroyed. Some SA-10 64N6 "Tomb-stone" installations, the most advanced SAM battery type the enemy was fielding, remained untouched. A Fata Morgana of missiles, one minute the batteries were there, the next they weren't.

The intel people surmised what was happening: The SAM commander knew his shit backward. He had trained his personnel to move rapidly and exploit the many rifts and defiles of the countryside in order to hide the mobile TELs carrying the SAMs. It was like a group of highly intelligent cockroaches on a

kitchen countertop scurrying for cover when the light
came on. There was only one way to take out Count
Dracula, and that was to land a recon force on the
ground.

That mission, according to Brigadier General "Patient K." Kullimore, had Cobra Force's name written
all over it. Unlike others in the MEU, Kullimore's
handle matched his personality. Patient K. was not
one to charge into action or send any of his men into
a meat grinder without first running the numbers.
Kullimore was a technician, dedicated to mastery of
the digital battlefield, and a tactical innovator. He
would never use a sword when a scalpel would do.
Patient K. judged Cobra Force the right scalpel for
the job. SACEUR and the Joint Chiefs backed him
up, and Cobra Force got itself a mission.


The Osprey's approach to the landing zone jarred
Chicken Wire awake. He'd been nodding off,
dreaming about a Russian stripper he'd once dated
named Svetlana. He remembered one of the FNGs
telling him to go fuck himself after he asked about
the guy named Pussy, but that was all. Now C.W.
shook the cobwebs from his head as the convertiplane's monster paddle blade prop-rotors slanted upward and the V-22 transitioned into standard helo
mode as it slowed over the clearing in the rugged
mountain country.

Navigating by means of forward-looking infrared
imaging, the pilot dropped the Osprey's underbelly to
within a few feet of the high mountain meadow that

was its destination, but kept the rotors dishing.

Minutes later, Cobra Force and its gear was on the ground and the Osprey was rising straight up like a freight elevator to transit from the LZ.

Once in theater, the team formed up and mud-checked its equipment, including the ITDs, or integrated tactical displays, strapped to their heads under their Fritz helmets.

The ITDs incorporated night vision imaging with digital graphics linked to small tactical computers carried on the team's webbing. The ITD system could also uplink to Defense Department satellites and unmanned air vehicles, and to surveillance and control aircraft like AWACS and JSTARS.

Cobra Force marched out of the LZ with color-coded moving map displays overlaying the monochrome low-light imagery of the surrounding terrain. The maps were keyed to Global Positioning System (GPS) satellites and had the unit's mission route already programmed in. Waypoints, indicated by circles, highlighted Objectives Victor, Whiskey, X-ray and Yankee amid the complex of hills and crags, ravines and valleys.

Analysts at NPIC, the CIA's National Photographic Interpretation Center, guessed that these were the most likely places Count Dracula might be holing up between SAM launches. Cobra Force's job was to hunt for the Count's TELs, and destroy them in place. The same Osprey that had ferried the unit into the op zone was ready to fly back in and pick up the team once the mission was accomplished.

But Chicken Wire didn't like the way it felt. His

grandfather had been a Marine on Iwo Jima, and from what C.W. remembered about what he'd been told, this country was a lot like Iwo. Only it wasn't an island, was considerably more forested and was way farther west of Japan.

Same type of broken topography, though, hills and gullies and ravines. In short, the ideal place for an enemy to hide in and, if need be, defend.

The experts didn't know shit from a hole in the ground. Seeing the terrain from an air-conditioned office was a hell of a lot different than seeing it with your dick plowing a furrow in the mud. Chicken Wire figured there could be more demons lurking beneath the surface than just the caves that the techs and wonks figured some of the TELs were being moved into for shelter.

It wasn't beyond the realm of possibility for there to be tunnels and bunkers sunk inside those hills too, chock-full of troops. Hell, you could hide a division in this countryside if you kept it well-hidden underground.

C.W. had brought that up during pre-mission briefings, but had been shot down. No indications of deep underground facilities were found. Where you had DUFs you also had to have ventilation shafts, access roads, comms transmitters. Where you had those you had TEMPEST—transient electromagnetic pulse emanations—and plenty of IR leakage.

But there wasn't zip to indicate any of this in the ops zone. Not a millivolt of TEMPEST, not a thousandth of a degree of radiant heat energy that didn't come from Mother Nature herself. Chicken Wire still wasn't convinced. The so-called experts had been wrong plenty of times before. They sure as hell could be wrong again. As far as he was concerned, C.W. would go on the assumption that they were wrong this time too.

Until he was convinced of the contrary, Cobra Force's Meister of the Pig would keep a tight grip on his M60 GPMG and consider anything that moved a potential threat, including the wind. Somewhere out there, maybe real close, Count Dracula's TEL crews were dug in, waiting for daybreak and their orders to move out and set up shop in this rugged hill country.

Cobra Force knew the name of the game was to drop the hammer on Count Dracula before the renegade Serb commander found them himself. Each member of the unit had a gut feeling that before their 48-hour mission time ticked down to zero, one or the other would happen. Heads Cobra, tails Dracula. Like the outcome of every mission, it could all hang on the toss of a coin.

# chapter *two*

Cobra Force moved cautiously across the high mountain meadow. The southern Balkan landscape was almost alpine here, the earth slashed with crags and scoured with gullies.

The predawn air was bone-chillingly cold. Although the team wore thermally insulated vests and underclothing beneath their parkas, and protected their faces and hands with masks and gloves, they felt the chill bite through like a wolf's teeth.

The Osprey pilot watched the altimeter line of his console gauge as the hard-chargers filed from the tilt-rotor A/C's rear ramp. The convertiplane's copilot kept watch on the terrain through GEN IV night vision goggles.

In under five minutes Cobra Force was on the ground. Now hundreds of pounds lighter, the Osprey rose straight up, translated to horizontal flight at 60 feet and shot away from the LZ as fast as a gigantic gob of spit.

The pilot checked his fuel gauge and INS. All systems read green. They might even make it home from this one.

**M**ajor David Saxon unshipped his satcom and turned in the op's first situation report.

"Rattler is down." He spoke into the compact cell phone–sized comms unit whose spread-spectrum SINCGARS signal was uplinked to a Milstar satellite in low earth orbit. "Repeat. Rattler is down. Proceeding to rally point Ace."

"Affirmative, Rattler. Will inform Eagle. Good luck."

"Thanks. Out."

"Eagle" and "Mongoose" were the call signs, respectively, of Saxon's immediate superiors, General Kullimore and Colonel Pete Mayall. The general already would have been informed of Cobra's successful insertion by now and prepared for phase two of the operation.

Saxon slid the satcom back in the side pocket of his BDU pants. He slid the sound-suppressed Colt Commando SMG cradled on his chest into a slightly more comfortable position and rubbed his fingerless-gloved hands against the biting chill.

The other members of the team all had their gear arranged and were hunched down at the tree line awaiting Saxon's orders to heft their packs and start humping.

"Yo, Hirsh. Take point."

"Fuck it—again?"

"No, not fuck it. Walk it, Hirsh."

"Sure, boss. Hirsh walks point. Gotta remember that. Hirsh always fuckin' walks point."

"Berlin" Hirsh—so named for his Brooklyn accent that substituted "burl" for "boil" and "goil" for "girl"—checked his GPS readout for the pre-programmed route to the first waypoint as well as compass bearings. Then he rotated his lip mike into position and adjusted the lightweight ITD goggles on his head. The darkness opened up to reveal a light-amplified image of the surrounding trees and under-brush.

"Mike check," Hirsh whispered into the black button mike held a quarter inch from his mouth on a flexible band. "There was once a young goil from Nantucket, whose cunt was as wide as a bucket. She was terribly sad, till she met a young lad, with a dong that was shaped like—"

"Cut the anatomy lesson," Saxon snapped. "We hear you all right. Just walk your point and zip your lip."

"Yes, sir," Hirsh replied. "Fuckin'-A, sir."

He turned and skulked off into the forest at a slow, deliberate pace, his posture slightly hunched to di-minish his profile to potential hidden enemies, his trained eyes already scanning the terrain, the barrel of his assault weapon tracking right and left. The pla-toon moved out in a star configuration, each soldier assuming the same crouched, skulking gait as the point man's. They were spaced at twenty-foot intervals behind Hirsh, with C.W. bringing up the rear cradling Pauline, his trusty Pig, and chewing a dead cigar.

Saxon and Mooner were among the outriders, swinging out to sixty feet at either side of the Marines at the center to cover their flanks. It was a long way up to their hide site in the hills and first light wasn't very far off.

**B**rigadier General Kullimore walked south along Corridor Six on the second floor of the Pentagon, turning onto the central A-Ring. Cobra Force's commanding officer had spent the better part of the late morning briefing the Joint Chiefs in a medium-sized conference room on the second floor known to Pentagon personnel as the Tank.

The Chiefs regularly convened in the Tank to be briefed on all matters of business concerning the U.S. military establishment, from strategic threats in distant nations to new designs for thrust-vectoring jet fighter engines.

This morning Kullimore had conducted a Tank briefing on his operational strategy for the Marine Expeditionary Unit's deployment in the southern Balkans.

The occasion was somewhat unusual insofar as officers of lesser rank generally gave Tank briefings. But the Chiefs, including Chairman Buck Starkweather, were anxious to hear Patient K.'s brief today—especially since it concerned some secret materials.

Befitting Kullimore's rank, the Chiefs dropped their traditional stony stares reserved for subordinates and relaxed as a fellow ranking officer addressed them. Kullimore's superior, Marine Commandant General Maxwell Caine, was especially interested, and peppered him with questions concerning the MEU's activities in theater.

Caine's Marine battalions were engaged in operations critical to the success of NATO efforts to uproot the resurgent Soviets and their Bulgarian allies from the southern Balkans, especially to dislodge their steadily growing foothold on Macedonia.

Patient K. answered Caine's questions and concluded his brief with a request for any final questions from the rest of the gathered Chiefs.

There were none.

The Chiefs and Deputy Chiefs thanked Kullimore for a good brief and dismissed him. As an old Pentagon hand, Patient K. still felt some of the nervousness of the young major who had delivered his first Tank brief more than twenty years before. But it passed quickly as he hurried along Corridor Six toward the A-Ring, catching an elevator whose doors were just closing.

Matters awaited him one floor up, and these now took over his thoughts.

The Marines Special Operations Command Center (MSOCC) on the third floor of the Pentagon was part of the complex of situation rooms making up the U.S. National Military Command Center (NMCC).

The Marines command center, a large central room with walls dominated by large flat panel display screens, was flanked by several other rooms for staff personnel. Only those holding A-level security clearances could gain admittance to the spec ops command center, and only a handful of personnel held such clearances.

The MP sentry on duty outside the door of the command center crisply saluted as Patient K. entered the room. As usual, a muted roar filled it, the product of humans and the machines they tended interacting under constantly changing combat situations.

The computers and communications links feeding into the MSOCC brought breaking real-time tactical information from the four corners of the globe. The links included SPINTCOM data from arrays of surveillance satellites that informed U.S. military personnel within two minutes of events anywhere in the world. The MSOCC was the nerve center of a far-flung network of invisible tie-lines to Marine forces on land, sea and air.

General Kullimore's executive officer, Colonel Mike Marner, spotted him coming in. The XO quickly stood from his desk and walked over.

"Sir," he said. "A satcom report from Rattler."

"In my office, Mike."

Marner followed Kullimore to a smaller side room at the corner of the large enclosure, closed the door and took a seat facing the desk at his boss's instructions.

"Well, what have you got?"

"Sir, Major Saxon's special mission detachment has entered the area of operations. The team's first sitrep indicated that they had marched from the LZ to rally point Ace and were in position."

"Anything else?"

"No sir," Marner answered. "Just that. Otherwise there were no problems reported. It's assumed everything is a go."

Kullimore leaned back in his chair and steepled his fingers beneath his chin, a sign to Marner that he was deep in thought. Marner knew he was considering his next decision.

It was a decision that would create new dangers for the personnel on the ground and have a potential effect on the entire scope of operations in the southern Balkan theater.

Marner waited, glancing at one of the elephants the general had decorating his office. Some were jade, others metal, others papier-mâché. Symbols of patience, all; the general's trademark.

It might have grated, but those elephants weren't the only tokens of the general's sangfroid. His grace under fire had earned Kullimore the Silver Star and Congressional Medal of Honor in Vietnam. The XO had grown accustomed to the ways of his boss and stayed cool while Kullimore deliberated.

Marner, a West Pointer, had been the general's XO for three years and he'd come to admire Kullimore as all those who knew him did. Marner had stayed on longer than most did at the Pentagon.

His stint as a staff officer was about to end—he

had already received his reassignment to training staff at Guantánamo. He would miss the Puzzle Palace when he left.

At last Patient K. sat forward in his chair and rested his unflinching gaze on Marner.

"Plan Welding Arc is to commence at once," he said. "Tell them down in the hole."

"Yes sir," Marner replied.

Kullimore was already at the keyboard of the computer terminal at his desk, entering the written orders into the system, where they would be passed to the appropriate personnel along the chain of command.

T hey called Colonel Vuc Dragunovic "Count Dracula" behind his back. Dragunovic knew all about the nickname. In fact, he was proud of it.

Vuc's family roots were in the Carpathian mountains of neighboring Romania, and one of his remote ancestors was indeed said to have been Vlad the Impaler. Tales of werewolves and forest demons had filled his childhood, related to him in utter seriousness by his parents in the small village of Volin.

His parents had crossed the border in the early days of the Cold War in order to escape the brutal Soviet-style dictatorship of Nicolae Ceauşescu. Ethnic Serbs, they had found life simpler in Marshal Tito's socialist republic.

Just the same, they were poor and never managed to crawl out of poverty. They had left Romania with little beside the clothes on their backs, the bundles lashed to their cart and the horse that pulled it across the border. Their grinding poverty was a curse to the young Vuc, and as he grew to manhood his hatred of it only increased.

To escape it, Dragunovic joined the Yugoslavian army, finding a home among the many Serbs who served in the ranks with him. Vuc's naturally violent inclinations found useful channels in the profession of arms and he rose quickly in the ranks. He was a major when Slobodon Milošović harangued his countrymen to revolt, and his passions were inflamed like all the other Serbs in the crowd.

Dragunovic went about the business of ethnic cleansing with relish. He was so good at his work that he was promoted to lieutenant colonel. His Serb patrols ranged throughout Bosnia and Herzegovina rounding up the enemy and putting their homes and villages to the torch.

Dragunovic earned his nickname then, taking pleasure in subjecting the leaders of the resistance and other enemy cadre to humiliating tortures. Dracula once more became a name to be feared, and along with Milosovic and many others, eventually placed on The Hague tribunal's international war criminals list.

Although Dragunovic did not play an active part in the second round of Serbian ethnic cleansing in Kosovo years later, he waited on the fringes. By this time, a full colonel, he had switched to artillery and commanded a secure outpost within Macedonia. The operation had added to the plundered wealth he had already amassed.

In his remote forested corner, Dragunovic reaped

the rewards of being in the dead center of a smuggling route that stretched from the opium fields of Iran up through Turkey, across the Aegean Sea and into Greece and Bulgaria. At its other end were the Western European nations and the British Isles.

Dragunovic's duty station gave him the means to amass great wealth, most of it socked away in numbered bank accounts in Switzerland and the Bahamas. The rebirth of the Soviet Union and the push of the Bulgarians into Macedonia only enriched him more, for now there was an even greater demand for the clandestine weapons he ran up from sources in the Arab countries and Israel.

The Serb commander didn't consider the games he played as motivated by greed but by survival. Algerian warlords and Chinese nationalist generals of previous wars had seen it the same way. They'd known they were on the losing side and prepared for the day when they would have to disappear over the border. Sackfuls of money were needed for that, escape routes had to be prepared and officials had to be bribed.

So they smuggled—diamonds, heroin, arms. It didn't matter what. As long as the cash and the goods flowed in and out. Count Dracula was playing the same game. Tonight's shipment would drop another peanut in his sack.

The multikilo load of Turkish heroin had just come in overland. The load had begun its journey by boat from the craggy headlands of the northeastern Turkish coast and crossed the Aegean Sea by night. It had traveled by SUV across Greece. At the Macedonian frontier border guards on both sides had been paid off. The load traveled the rest of the way by four-wheel-drive truck.

Dracula had one of his people inspect the load for purity. When he got the nod the money changed hands. The blindfolds that had kept the location of the Serb's underground base secret from the drug runners were put back on again, and the Greeks were driven back to the spot where the commando force had met them.

They were honest brokers. The merchandise was high quality. Dracula would continue doing business with them. He hoped they understood that the minute they tried to fuck him, they were dead.

## chapter *three*

The F/A-18F Super Hornets shot from the fore-deck of the Nimitz class carrier *Eisenhower* lying off the Adriatic coast on a catapult of high-pressure steam.

Their mission called for a short burn to gain altitude and rendezvous with a tanker to top off their tanks with avgas. They were then to fly a high level vector due east across Albania and Macedonia, drop their ordnance, then turn around and head back.

The pilots, backseaters and wingmen were instructed that they were on a bombing mission to take out SAMs in the mountains of Macedonia. This was a contrivance; indeed, a deliberate deception.

The true purpose of the fighter sortie was known only to high-ranking officers and key U.S. intelligence analysts. If the Hornets killed any SAMs, that was icing on the cake. But it wasn't the cake itself. Not by a long shot.

The pilot of the lead Super Hornet confirmed by radio to the wingman cruising just off his right that they had reached the initial point for release of munitions loadout. Cockpit instruments had already advised the aircrew of the sortie's arrival at the IP.

The planes carried a mix of weapons including long-range AMRAAMs and JDAM equipped bombs. They also carried Sidewinders for use against hostile aircraft. The fighters would take the first target group from standoff range using the AMRAAMs. Uncaging the Advanced Medium Range Air-to-Air Missiles, the crew turned over the first stage of guided flight to the automated targeting systems of the planes and the missiles themselves.

The WSOs on board the F/A-18s were about to pickle off the ordnance when their threat warning radars suddenly went berserk. Surface-to-air missiles had been fired at the fighters and were now speeding their way. The aircrew fired off the AMRAAMs and broke formation as soon as the birds were loosed, hoping to outrun the pursuing SAMs.

The flight leader managed to successfully outmaneuver the tracking missile by jinks, turns and other evasive flight tactics, and by using electronic countermeasures. The lead plane's crew breathed with relief as it saw the bright flash light up the sky to their left, indicating where the SAM warhead had exploded harmlessly in midair.

The other F/A-18 wasn't as fortunate.

The pilot had almost succeeded in shaking off the

second SAM that had chased the Hornet doggedly across the skies. Chaff and flares had been popped to foil SAM radar and IR tracking and the pilot executed a fast break-turn to fly out of harm's way.

The SAM seemed unfazed, however. It doggedly continued tracking and exploded within a few hundred yards of the aircraft.

The pilot ejected as shrapnel from the warhead ripped through the fuselage, tearing into the cockpit. Although the backseater had been killed almost instantly, the pilot didn't know it until it became evident that no other chute had opened anywhere in the sky.

Saxon personally took the satcom message. The full global-mobile comms pack had been set up at Cobra's second rally point, and the force had video as well as audio links to the MSOCC. Their contact, Colonel Marner, was at the other end of the real-time connection.

"There's been a snag," Marner reported. "An F/A-18 pilot is down in your vicinity. We need your people to see if you can pick him up before the opposition finds him."

"He ejected safely?"

"As far as we know, yes," Marner asserted. "The location of the crash area is about fifty statute miles from your position. We estimate your team can reach it before daylight. Any reason why you couldn't?"

Saxon thought it over a moment. Rescuing downed fliers wasn't his people's job. That was a mission for

Delta and other rescue formations, who were trained for the mission. Besides, Cobra Force already had its orders. Yet Marner was the old man's XO and Saxon assumed with good reason that the new orders came directly from Patient K.

"No reason. We're good to go."

"Affirmative," Marner replied. "The pilot is transmitting on SINCGARS distress frequency Blue. See if you can establish direct communications."

"Roger. How does this impact on Welding Arc?" Saxon asked.

A cornerstone of the mission planning had been for the Super Hornets to lure Dracula's TELs out into the open and entice them into taking a few shots at the fighter aircraft. In order to do this they also would have to turn on the search and tracking radars on the missile launchers.

It was an enticement to what the Pentagon planning cell called EMCON suicide—a form of lethal chicken with radar emissions. With emission control (EMCON) temporarily gone, an orbiting RC-135 electronic surveillance aircraft would be stationed to pick up the electrons cast by the SAM radars.

Higher up, in low earth orbit, a Maverick signals intelligence (SIGINT) satellite, or "ferret bird," would absorb and read the emissions from another perspective. The combined fingerprints of enemy radar would help direct Cobra Force toward Dracula's hiding places, wherever they might be, so that the Marines special ops detail could destroy the TELs in position.

Saxon realized that the downing of the Super Hornet might have scrubbed the mission, or at least degraded their overhead coverage.

"We're still analyzing ferret bird and RC-135 data," Marner advised. "We got some during the SAM launches and maybe it'll be enough. The mission may not be compromised. First we want the pilot, and we want to make sure no black boxes fall into the hands of unfriendlies."

"Black boxes" did not refer to commercial airlines' flight data recorders, which were neither really black nor boxy, but more commonly egg-shaped and brightly painted to be easily seen from a distance. Major Saxon understood Marner's reference to black boxes to be the military meaning: classified military electronics modules that controlled various functions of the aircraft, including communications, countermeasures, radar and avionics.

The Super Hornet was one of the most advanced fighter planes in the skies, and some considered it more high-tech than the Air Force's coveted F-22 Raptor. Saxon knew that various forms of active stealth and weapons subsystems contained in black boxes aboard the F/A-18 would be spirited away for reverse engineering if they chanced to fall into enemy hands.

"You are to locate the remains of the aircraft and destroy any classified components of the airframe or avionics. Should most of the airframe remain intact, you are to blow it up."

"That's affirm."

"Good luck, major," Marner replied. "At your next scheduled sitrep we should have hopefully sorted out the SIGINT data. At that time, we can also make arrangements to helo-extract the pilot if he's still alive."

The window on the laptop screen went blank. Saxon had received his orders. Now the rest of the team would receive theirs in turn.

Saxon turned to his troop.

"Da Noiz, Hirsh. We got us a job. Get your gear together. We move out in ten."

"How come the rest of us don't get to play?" Mooner asked.

"Because you forgot to put on your deodorant this morning. You guys stay here at the hide site. If we need you we'll holler."


The three-man buddy team had been humping through the cold mountain countryside for an hour before Saxon told them to take ten. He wanted to find out if the pilot could be raised on the radio. They had tried making contact earlier using Blue and other distress fequencies without luck.

"Still nobody home, boss," Da Noiz told Saxon, taking the compact satcom-capable communicator from his ear and sliding it into its pouch on his combat webbing.

"Nothing at all?" Saxon asked.

"Nothing, boss. Just a bunch of freakin' static."

Saxon looked around him. He sat with his back up against the trunk of a very tall tree. The second-growth forest was dense; the pine, fir and maple grew thickly together and blocked out much of the sunlight.

As Saxon peered up, he squinted at the pinwheels of bright sunlight that formed an ever-changing pattern of flickering lights between the rustling branches.

The treetop canopy, Saxon reflected, would be an ideal place to position snipers on hidden platforms. Well-trained teams of snipers, sited at random positions inside the forest, could remain in place for days on end. If properly outfitted they could be virtually invisible from the ground.

The original plan had factored in the possible presence of snipers, but the team's movements had been planned to avoid densely forested areas. Now, with the sudden orders to rescue the downed pilot, Saxon was aware that he was subjecting himself and his personnel to a heightened level of danger, and one that the team had not been specifically outfitted or trained to contend with.

Still, the buddy team was trained to move quietly and alertly in forest environments, and they would be difficult to see and hear except at extremely close range. The team wore NATO woodland camouflage gear, its mottled pattern breaking up their silhouettes to any hidden observers that might lurk in the woods.

Saxon, Da Noiz and Hirsh had cammied up their faces, and draped their helmets with gillie cover. Elastic camo wrappings were also pulled around their Commando assault weapons.

Not only did the wrappings help conceal the silenced, full-automatic bullpups, but they also muffled the giveaway clink, clatter and rattle of metal fastenings on the guns that could reveal their presence to unfriendly patrols.

Saxon had no doubt that there were patrols in the sector. The Serb commander called Dracula was too wily a contender not to have reconnaissance teams out walking the perimeter. Booby traps and mines in the forest were also a realistic possibility.

But Saxon decided that the main concern on the rescue mission would come from booby traps and any unexpected encounters with unfriendly patrols, not snipers. Dracula was probably out searching for the remains of the aircraft and would have his own dragnets combing the woods.

Saxon got up and cradled his short-barreled Commando assault weapon. Hirsh and Da Noiz needed no further prompting to understand that the rest break was over. They too rose and prepared to leave the small clearing, their eyes and ears scanning the surrounding forest terrain as they adjusted their gear and cradled their sound-suppressed guns.

A t the team's hide site, the rest of the unit was occupied with setting up a remote reconnaissance mission. The base station was linked by Land Warrior digital technology to satellites in orbit that could relay communications in near–real time via an over-the-horizon satellite relay capability over the orbital Milstar net.

The net not only enabled Cobra Force ground combat personnel to download satellite intelligence on reconnaissance targets, it also allowed them to control remote piloted vehicles when they needed a closer or more detailed look at a particular surveillance target.

This was the case right now at the hide site. The small recess—not even deep enough to be termed a cavern—in the mountainside that the team had chosen as its hide site/command post had been outfitted with an array of miniature remote sensors, low-light cameras and communications antennas. All were camouflaged; and the cameras and sensors were engineered so that their thermal signatures were reduced.

Feeder cables hidden under leaves and dirt snaked inside the recess and were linked to the portable computer system manned by Pfc. Bart "Doctor" Jeckyll, the team's technical and communications specialist. Nestled in a shockproof milspec case, the portable computer's large, flat-panel display had two windows open on it.

One window was a view from low earth orbit as a KH-12 Improved Crystal photographic intelligence (PHOTINT) satellite tracked the progress of a Tier III+ unmanned aerial vehicle en route to the southern Balkans. The second window was currently blank except for a digital time display that ticked off the hours, minutes and seconds. In only a few more minutes, the Tier III+ UAV, known as Global Hawk, would be within range and be remotely controllable by Jeckyll.

Global Hawk was a thirteen-ton aircraft the size of a single-engine plane with a 116-foot wingspan. Its fuselage blended seamlessly into a huge ramjet intake at the rear and flared into a rounded sensor bulge at the front, with long, slightly backswept glider wings sprouting from the hull's midsection. The combination of design elements gave the robot plane the look of a winged monster blindworm imbued with cold, sinister intelligence—which was not very far from the truth.

Global Hawk was built to fly long endurance missions that required it to stay airborne—or, in military parlance, "loiter"—for as much as twenty-five hours before returning to base. During that time it could aerially survey approximately forty thousand square nautical miles, a target area equivalent to the state of Illinois, with a resolution of objects as small as three feet in diameter.

Utilizing spot-mode scanning, it could surveil a much smaller area with a resolution of objects down to one foot in size, if necessary. The UAV was also equipped to carry EO (electronic intelligence) and SAR (synthetic aperture radar) imaging payloads as well as a third IR system simultaneously while operating at altitudes of greater than sixty thousand feet.

The UAV was crammed with a ton of cameras, radars and other sensors. All of that gear was now under Jeckyll's total control.

Shit hot, he thought as he began to maneuver Tier III+ by a small joystick attached to the keyboard of the portable computer unit.

Single file, each man widely spaced about twenty feet behind the one in front, Saxon's team moved cautiously through the forest underbrush, negotiating the hilly terrain at a careful snail's pace.

Hirsh walked point. The team navigated by means of GPS, which indicated that only a little more than two kilometers separated them from the crash site of the downed F/A-18.

The buddy team looked out for the smell of smoke, distant sounds that might indicate hostile forces picking through the wreckage or other signs of unfriendlies in the vicinity.

So far there was no break in the natural patterns of sights, sounds and smells of the woodland environment that surrounded the Cobra team.

Saxon considered the stocky Brooklynite the best point man he'd ever worked with. Hirsh used his eyes and ears, but he also had an almost sixth sense for hidden dangers that had proven its worth over the course of the missions Cobra had been assigned. Where the city boy got it from, Saxon, a rural West Virginian, didn't know, but there was no doubt that he had the instincts of a bloodhound.

Da Noiz walked behind Hirsh while Saxon brought up the rear. The three Marines were attuned to the overall environment, scanning ground, perimeter and the treetop canopy overhead for concealed threats.

They continued to see nothing amiss when Hirsh held up his hand and made swiveling motions with his wrist, pointing downward. The other two Marines worked their way toward Hirsh's position, at the top of a shallow rise in the forest floor.

Following where Hirsh was pointing, down into a wooded hollow, they saw the shattered, twisted wreckage of a jet fighter, strewn across the landscape.

It lay undisturbed in the eerie silence of the forest.

There was no indication that anyone besides themselves had discovered it yet. There was no sign of the pilot either.

chapter *four*

The buddy team negotiated the debris field where the plane had broken up on impact. The caustic odor of burnt aviation gasoline filled the air here and the area showed the signs of fire damage. The plane had come down like a meteor, showering burning wreckage all around.

"Listen up," Saxon told Hirsh and Da Noiz. "I want to conduct a fast search for the black boxes. When you find them disable them with the thermite charges we brought along."

"We hear ya, boss," both men answered, almost in unison.

"Keep your eyes peeled."

"Gotcha."

Saxon covered the other two men as they prowled among the debris field in the depression. The going would be made considerably simpler for the team because much of the aircraft's fuselage was still intact. Thermite charges would take care of that too.

The chemical incendiary agent generated extremely high temperatures without explosion. A thermite charge of sufficient strength would cut through hardened steel plate like an acetylene torch with minimal sound.

Saxon keyed his comms. "We've reached the debris field," he told Jeckyll at the hide site. "Hirsh and Da Noiz are searching for Rheingold and Budweiser. Any company in sight?"

"Negit, boss," Jeckyll replied, scanning multispectral feed from the unit's dedicated Tier III+, scrolling from video to infrared to synthetic aperture radar displays. "Overhead surveillance shows no unfriendly movement in your vicinity."

"That's affirm," Saxon replied. "Let me know if there's any change."

"Good to go, boss," Jeckyll told him.

Saxon keyed squelch and continued to scan the perimeter. The pilot had to be nearby, but where exactly? The flyboy had to have been aware that he couldn't have gotten very far on foot.

Just then Saxon heard a shrill cue-tone in his earbud.

"Boss, we found 'em," Hirsh said over comms.

"You're sure they're the right ones?"

"Positive. The serial numbers match and everything else checks out."

"Roger. Set the charges for one-minute detonation

delays. We'll need to visually confirm they've been destroyed before we leave the area."

Saxon watched the two men work a short distance away. Crouched over the two secret modules of U.S. Navy electronics, they unpacked thermite charges, digital timers and electrical blast initiators.

Saxon wondered what exactly was inside those things. They were supposed to be guidance and avionics packages, but that could be a bunch of bullshit. When you dealt with spooks and brass you generally got the mushroom treatment: kept in the dark and fed crap. Not that he gave a damn. They could be packed with the president's dirty laundry for all he cared. His orders were to destroy those modules, and that was what he'd do.

Hirsh and Da Noiz rose from their crouches and Hirsh raised his arm in a thumbs-up. They were ready to roll. The two Marines hustled for the shelter of some lichen-encrusted boulders nearby. The timers were already spinning their numbers.

Saxon silently counted down to zero, shading his eyes with his hand against the bright flash when the thermite charges reached their ignition flashpoints. The charges only took a few seconds to do its work. The black boxes could not withstand the intense heat thermite generated.

"We got two pieces of melted junk here, boss," Da Noiz reported in a few moments. The deed was done.

"Okay. We're out of here," Saxon said into his lipmike.

The team formed up and humped away from the crash site and debris field. The next part of the assignment was to find the pilot. Saxon wondered if he were dead or comatose, or badly injured on ejection. He might still be alive, somewhere out there.

Some minutes later, Da Noiz, out ahead on point, broke in on comms.

"Boss, I got a chute and harness hanging in a tree over here," he reported.

"Any sign of the pilot?"

"Negative. I'm continuing to search."

Cradling his silenced autoweapon, Saxon looked up at the sky—or tried to—through the forest canopy. The closely spaced timber continued to obscure everything except broken patches of blue and dazzling bursts of sunlight.

He knew that somewhere above them, up to its 30,000-foot ceiling, the Tier III+ UAV was orbiting, its sensors scanning the terrain below out to a radius of scores of miles.

Saxon keyed his comms.

"Whatcha got?"

"Still nothing to report, boss," Jeckyll replied. "No indication of unfriendly movement in your vicinity. No sign of the pilot. The situation remains unchanged."

"Contact Eagle. Tell them we've taken care of Rheingold and Budweiser. Out."

Saxon broke off. Everything was good to go, but he was still gripped by a sense of uneasiness. This didn't add up right. There was no reason to doubt the absence of Serb patrols as reported by Tier III+. They were in the midst of some of the most remote and rugged mountain country in the southern Balkans.

There was little reason for the breakaway Macedonian-Serb government in Skopje to establish fixed defensive perimeters here. Random patrols would be enough to provide security coverage. Likewise, the locations of most of the mobile SAM launchers in the belt were known to NATO, and none were in Cobra's immediate vicinity.

This was virgin timber country, without roads of any kind, making it impossible for the lumbering launch vehicles of mobile SAMs to maneuver in. Saxon chalked up his unease to a case of nerves.

A series of musical electronic chirps sounded in Saxon's ear. It was Da Noiz reporting in.

"Lissen up. I found the pilot."

"What's his condition?" asked Saxon, suddenly alert and focused. "Does he need medical attention?"

"No. The pilot's uninjured."

"Tell him to keep his shirt on," Saxon said. "We'll arrange to helivac him out of here."

Da Noiz looked at the pilot and smiled at what Saxon had just told him. "Affirmative," he said. "Out."

Saxon and Hirsh reached the pilot's location a short while later.

"Holy Jesus, it's a broad," Hirsh blurted.

"Where'd this refugee from a William Bendix movie come from?" the pilot asked.

"Flatlands Avenue and East 35th Street," Hirsh answered. "That's in Brooklyn."

"I said she should keep her shirt on, boss," Da Noiz related. "Just like you told me."

"I'm Major Saxon. I'm in command," Saxon said to the flier. "Who are you?"

"Brennan," she answered. "Lieutenant Colleen Brennan. 1st Marine Aviation Air Wing, Fifth Fighter Attack Squadron. Off the *Eisenhower*. I hear you guys found my plane."

"Yeah. Wasn't much left of it, though," Hirsh told Brennan.

"We're arranging transport for you. You'll be back aboard the carrier in no time. A V-22 is already en route. We need to hustle to a clearing nearby that the helo can use as an LZ."

The clearing, a high meadow edged with sparse clusters of trees, was about a quarter mile distant from the crash site. The team, with Brennan in tow, reached it after a short hump through the uneven, hilly forest terrain.

To save time they had rappelled up a steep, rocky hill slope. Saxon had ordered Da Noiz and Hirsh to haul Brennan up but the woman pilot had insisted on rappelling herself up to the top. She wasn't trained for the ascent, and it showed, but Saxon was relieved when she completed the climb under her own steam.

He'd be glad to be rid of her, not because she was a woman, but because she didn't have the training and probably didn't have the moves to be part of

Cobra Force. The team had other business in the field and had already been slowed up enough by having to sidetrack to the pilot's rescue.

A double-note chime sounded in Saxon's earbud. It was Jeckyll on the comms link.

"The CH-53 reports it is en route with no anticipated delay," Cobra's technical whiz reported. "I have an ETA of ten minutes. The cockpit crew wants to know if you're gonna be ready to transfer the passenger onto the helo when they arrive."

"We're positioned at the LZ and ready to hand off the pilot to the CH-53's aircrew. No problems or delays are anticipated."

"That's affirm," Jeckyll said back. "I'll let the chopper know."

Saxon turned back to the team. Announcing the ETA for the helo, he deployed Hirsh and Da Noiz on the perimeter as defensive lookouts. Hunkering in the grass and in a stand of cedar, the two Marines quickly disappeared amid the woodland foliage, positioned where they could cover the entire meadow from their well-concealed vantage points.

Saxon and Brennan crouched on the perimeter at a position at three o'clock to the other hidden Marines. When the chopper came in, Saxon would move her out under cover of their weapons and hand her off to the Sea Stallion's aircrew.

Brennan hadn't tried to make conversation while they waited and Saxon didn't encourage it; in fact, he was glad of the silence. It helped him concentrate on his job. He didn't like being around women in combat situations.

Regardless of how capable they might be as soldiers, there was too much of an instinct in the male to protect the female, too much of the chivalrous knight in most men, and that propensity clouded thinking.

Centuries before, the Amazons had fought alongside the Celts and Druids opposing the Roman legions. The women had fought well, but most of the battles went to the all-male cohorts of Rome.

Maybe there was a lesson in that for America too. You could care about your buddy, but you could stay cold at the core and keep your mental and emotional distance. With a woman, something else was always getting in the way, either your prick or your head. Either way it went spelled trouble on the battlefield.

Saxon scanned the sky and checked his chronometer. The inbound chopper was due any time now. A transmission from the hide site confirmed: Jeckyll reported that the helo was only a few klicks from their position; arrival was imminent.

Saxon strained his ears and thought he heard the faint sound of churning rotors echoing off the surrounding ridgelines. Seconds later there was no doubt. The CH-53 appeared above the encircling peaks and burst into view like a big, slow-moving bullet.

Saxon pulled a smoke canister from his tactical vest, yanked off the cotter pin and popped green smoke in the center of the clearing. The pilot in the helo saw the smoke and edged the chopper close to the landing zone that Saxon had marked out for him.

"Let's shake it," Saxon told Brennan.

Soon he and the pilot were running across the meadow toward the flaring chopper.

They had gone midway toward the center of the clearing when they were suddenly taking fire. The whole world seemed to explode as gouts of earth and pulverized rubble cascaded skyward. The noise and muzzle flashes were deafening and disorienting.

Saxon immediately dropped down and flung Brennan to one side. Another explosion came from off to their left, somewhere behind the trees.

Mortars, Saxon told himself.

Amidst the unholy din Saxon recognized the telltale sound of some major bad shit about to happen. He knew what loomed on the horizon. A sun of pain and confusion was about to rise on them and light up a world of hurt.

More explosions confirmed Saxon's thought. Cobra Force was coming under heavy mortar attack.

Saxon looked up as the shelling momentarily ceased and the smoke cleared. Now a new sound had joined the infernal din. The chattering of a field machine gun from an emplacement somewhere off to his left had added its staccato note to the devil's symphony. Bullets were punching into the grass and pinging off large rocks and boulders, raising sparks and whirlpools of dust.

He still had no idea of where exactly the fire was originating from. It was close, though. Too damned close.

Then another sound joined the din of battle. Saxon recognized it at once and took heart. It was an ugly sound, but a friendly one; a lot uglier if you were on the wrong side. The sound came from overhead, and the special music it made told Saxon he was hearing the battle cry of one of the MAG L20A1 machine guns aboard the CH-53, churning out 7.62-mm rounds so fast that it seemed like one continuous stream of death.

Almost simultaneously, Saxon heard the sound of automatic small arms fire start up from behind and at four o'clock. There was the heavier, staccato reports of Kalashnikovs coming in answer from the opposite direction, then the sound of men screaming in pain.

The Kalashnikovs abruptly ceased as other men barked orders. Saxon smiled grimly. He knew the opposition—whoever they were—had not seen his pickets but that Hirsh and Da Noiz had seen them and had opened up on the Yugos as they crossed the field.

That was good news, but Saxon still cursed his luck. He was pinned down in the clearing and couldn't do a damn thing about it.

"What the hell's happening?" he asked over comms.

"A platoon of Yugos, boss." It was Jeckyll speaking. "They came up fast and somehow our UAV didn't get imagery on 'em. I've got the UAV at the top of its envelope right now in case they got Stingers to use against the helo."

"What's the enemy's disposition?"

"Mortar crew's set up on a ridge southwest of your position. The platoon's broken up into two squads, which are encircling the clearing. One squad's to your left, the other a little farther out on your right. But they didn't see our guys strung out in the tree line.

The Yugo soldier boys on the left got creamed. I count . . . two, three . . . six dead or severely wounded, altogether. Practically wiped out the whole fuckin' squad."

"Hirsh, Da Noiz—say your situation."

"Hangin' right in there, boss," Hirsh said back. "We—"

Another mortar salvo hit nearby and the earth shook and thundered under the impact of the blast. Hirsh's words were blotted out in the earsplitting din of a high explosive strike. Saxon knew that the enemy was walking his fire. The Yugo forces out there were trying to get his people taped.

"Shit—say again, Hirsh."

"We got most of them motherfuckers. The rest look like they're trying to regroup."

"Jeckyll, any indication of reinforcements?"

"Negative so far."

Another mortar round struck home with a loud *ca-rump*. Saxon wished he could somehow reach out and crush that emplacement on the hill. He hated mortars, as did every mud-eating infantry soldier.

Now the chopper's MAG guns chattered again. The helo turned; the rear ramp gunner drew a bead and launched a salvo of rotoring death down into the enemy ranks. There again came the sound of Yugo infantry screaming and dying amid the din of multiple explosions as mortar cans and ammo stores cooked off.

Suddenly Saxon spotted a Yugo squad trying to make its way toward their position, creeping and hunch-walking across the open space, alternately run-

ning and dropping behind whatever cover the rocky
terrain surface afforded.

Saxon realized he and Brennan were pinned down
without much cover against a mobile and numerically
superior enemy maneuvering to outflank and encircle.
He needed better cover before the Yugos trapped
them and dropped a shell right down their throats.
Saxon spotted a rocky outcropping not far away that
would provide better cover than what they currently
had.

Reaching down he yanked two mini-grenades off
his modular lightweight load system (MOLLE) webbing. Pulling the cotter pin from first one, then the
other, he flung the armed grenades at the approaching
enemy squad in rapid succession. The twin blasts
killed at least one of the troopers, possibly injured
another.

Yelling curses, other enemy soldiers stood up and
charged. Saxon was already sighting on them, firing
three-round Commando bursts from a combat crouch.
He hammered the oncoming Yugos with controlled
automatic fire, stopping and emptying his clip before
he and Brennan ran for fresh cover. Sprawled in the
dirt, breathing hard, Saxon snapped in a fresh clip
and recharged the weapon.

The chopper swung over and the right door gunner
got what was left of the second Yugo infantry unit.
Jeckyll had switched the field unit's comms into an
open SINCGARS net so they could communicate directly with the Sea Stallion.

"We're going after the mortar pit," the pilot radioed. "Back for you soon."

The chopper swung over the bloodied meadow. There was still sporadic firing coming from the few Yugo survivors in the field, but the three Marines and Brennan, who had retained her service pistol, would be enough to take them out.

The mortar rounds still came sailing in from the Yugo emplacement, and they were getting dangerously closer. But the mortar crew's life expectancy was numbered by minutes and rapidly approaching the zero mark.

The helo swept across the meadow, gained altitude and approached the mortar position. It hovered in the air while its gun crew reloaded and got ready for another go-round at the enemy. As soon as the MAGs were loaded and recharged, the hellacious firing began again without letup.

The machine gunners cooked off every bullet on their belts, hosing down the mortar emplacement until raw firepower overwhelmed it. Suddenly there was a bright detonation flash, followed by a rapid, crackling string of secondary explosions as the cache of mortar ammunition ignited and went up.

The fight was over. "Hugo" was finished. Cracking gouts of flame licked up from the top of the ridgeline and a pall of black smoke coiled up slowly into the blue sky, to preside over the battlefield like a rearing cobra. No more mortar cans fell on the meadow.

The CH-53 came sweeping back to take care of any Yugo stragglers that might be left of the assault platoon, but by the time the helo reached the more open ground of the meadow, none of the unfriendlies remained alive. The leathernecks had seen to that.

Once the mortar pit was no longer active, the three Marines had broken from cover and become hunters instead of hunted. They had killed two enemy soldiers who fired back, but several more Yugos got up and waved their hands in the air. Hirsh and Da Noiz shot them anyway.

The Yugos fell to the ground with stunned expressions on their faces. They had never figured the Americans could be as utterly ruthless as they themselves were. It became their final lesson in life: Americans were not soft—the last thing they learned before a burst of 5.56mm bullets sent them straight to hell.

# chapter *five*

**T**he Yugo opposition force had been taken out but the presence of the Marine special operations detachment in the area was now compromised. Before or during the firefight somebody in the opposing force had radioed their HQ. That was a given. A guy in Yugo olive drab was probably working their plot on a grid map right now.

Brennan had been safely evacuated aboard the CH-53 Sea Stallion. Although the helo had sustained minor damage in the attack on the LZ, it was still airworthy.

The Cobra Force rescue element had watched the chopper rise straight into the air, reach its translation altitude of about sixty feet and then speed away toward the northeast until it vanished from sight.

Later the team would learn that the CH-53 had

safely landed with its passenger aboard the Nimitz class carrier USS *Eisenhower* off the southern Albanian coast and that its passenger was back in the air war.

Meanwhile, in the aftermath of the firefight, the three-man buddy team made a fast search of the unfriendly KIAs before they departed the field. The dead Yugos had seen the assault force from a distance and wanted to know more about their disposition. The dead wore the standard O.D. uniforms of Serbian regulars.

Their weapons were natively produced versions of the Soviet AKS-74 assault rifle. Looking into the faces of those who lay sprawled on their backs and turning over those who lay facedown in the dirt, Saxon saw the faces of young men who would have not long been out of basic training, or whatever passed for it in the Serb army. An NCO lying nearby looked somewhat older, but again, it was apparent to Saxon that these were mainly green troops.

Saxon guessed that the Cobra Force rescue element had been set upon by a random patrol. The patrol had gone ahead and attacked without waiting for reinforcements. Its assault tactics had been crude and poorly thought out. With the entrance into the fray of the Sea Stallion the outcome of the contest had been a foregone conclusion.

Saxon also had no doubt that the patrol had radioed their position and that more Yugo troops were en route to the area. Saxon acted quickly, forming up the team and issuing instructions.

They were to hole up in the woods until darkness

and then move out to link up with the base camp unit. The team at the hide site was also to break camp and march to a new rally point, Bravo.

They would then determine whether they could continue their primary mission or request extraction themselves. The shit was getting hot.

**T**he renegade Serb commander studied the transcript of the last radio transmission of the patrol. The patrol, Colonel Vuc Dragunovic noted, had engaged NATO troops in a firefight in the mountainous region near Kicevo.

Dragunovic knew the area well. It was a remote area of crags and rocky ridges, almost alpine in its terrain features. An excellent place, he mused, to covertly insert commando paratroop formations. The transmission reported the appearance of a helicopter before it broke off. There was no more after that partial transmission.

Colonel Dragunovic wrote off the patrol to NATO special forces troops. A larger patrol, of company strength, was already en route to the vicinity of the engagement, but Dragunovic had little doubt that it would find nothing but corpses when it arrived.

The colonel had expected one of the various special mission units formed by the NATO powers for some time and was not unduly alarmed that the expected intrusion had in fact taken place.

The Western nations had been training their elite units in tactics designed to hunt and destroy Scuds, SAMs and NBC weapons for almost a decade. Such a scalpel force, as they called it, had been used before. When the smart weaponry and the tactical strikes failed to wipe out these weapons the special forces elements were to be sent in.

Yet every countermove creates an opening for still another, oppositional countermove. The Moscow-Sofia axis had provided Dragunovic with a crack security force of Russian Spetsnaz intended to locate, track and annihilate any ground force that the NATO powers might insert into his mountain domain. His men were highly skilled and ruthless. They were as adept at hunting the Scud-killers as the Scud-killers were at hunting Scuds.

They were also well-paid, earning cash bounties for every enemy scalp they brought back to headquarters. In addition to the company of Yugo regulars, Dragunovic had already unleashed two squads of his ruthless Spetsnaz to hunt down the NATO special missions unit. He had no doubt that they would carry out their mission successfully.

For the moment, Dragunovic had other, more important, matters occupying his mind. The two couriers from Istanbul had run a double game on him. In Baghdad, at the other end of the delivery chain, there were some very unhappy and high-ranking military staff who were displeased with Dragunovic.

The colonel had been making a healthy profit trading Western weapons and missile technology for diamonds, gold and other valuable commodities. He had already amassed a small fortune, spread around the world in secure numbered bank accounts.

But money did you no good if you weren't alive

to spend it. Dragunovic did not want the Iraqis mad at him. That could prove unwise.

The screams of the two couriers echoed off the stone walls of the colonel's underground headquarters. Radom, his expert in interrogation, had been working on them for fifteen minutes already, and the cries of pain told Dragunovic that Radom had been working with his usual efficiency, some might even say artistry.

Dragunovic approached the prison section of the base and was admitted by an orderly who smartly saluted his commander.

He then walked along a narrow hallway lined with steel doors. Behind most of the doors were prison cells, hollows crudely excavated from the hard stone walls of the cavern complex, unventilated, unlighted and unheated against the often bitter mountain cold.

Dragunovic stopped to light a cigarette as he passed his private vale of tears and reflected that he would rather take his own life than pass a week in such a place. Yet there were wretches behind those solemn doors who had been imprisoned for months.

He had no idea how they managed to survive their imprisonment. Surely they understood that they would never leave here alive.

As Dragunovic inhaled the first drag of his American smoke, a flash of motion caught his eye. A prisoner was sticking his hands through the spaces between the bars of the small judas hole in one of the cell doors.

"Please, a cigarette," the prisoner begged in a weak voice. "Only a drag, I beg of you."

Dragunovic stepped closer, his eyes narrowing as he saw, in the gloom behind the door, the whiteness of a face pressed close to the bars. There was something familiar about the voice now, and even the small portion of face sparked recognition. Of course. He remembered the prisoner now.

"Good evening, colonel," Dragunovic said, addressing the gaunt, skull-like face. "It has been quite some time since we last met, hasn't it?"

He stepped back from the small barred window. The cell stunk and the stench was starting to reach him.

"Yes, it is I, Dragunovic. I whom you imprisoned and whose rank you usurped.

"I was under the impression you were dead, colonel," Dragunovic said, enjoying the sensation of cigarette smoke blowing through his nostrils in two thick streams. "You disappoint me. Why are you still alive? If you need help in dying, I will be happy to provide it."

"I am worse than dead," the prisoner croaked weakly. "You have confined me to a living purgatory."

Dragunovic smoked and regarded his prisoner. He took the red hard pack emblazoned with the American cowboy from his pocket and handed a cigarette to the prisoner, who clutched it with shaking fingers and brought it to his lips.

Dragunovic flipped back the cap of his lighter with a metallic snap and thumbed on the flame. The tip of the cigarette glowed orange as the prisoner dragged on it.

"Enjoy your smoke, colonel," Dragunovic told the prisoner and walked on.

He would make a note to have him executed at daybreak. He would make sure the firing squad had instructions to permit him a last smoke before he died, though. Let the wretch have his final dignity.

One of the few doors that did not have a narrow cell behind it was the one at the end of the corridor; the one from which the screams erupted in a steadily building crescendo.

Dragunovic rapped on the door, was scanned by a guard behind it, and admitted with a crisp salute. The commander strode into the large, dimly lit chamber behind the portal, the crack of his combat boot soles against the rock floor echoing off the cell's stone walls.

Like the prisoners' cells, the chamber had also been hewn from the living rock, but it was many times their size. This was the underground installation's interrogation chamber, a Hades presided over by Sergeant Radom Nikolic as its dark lord of pain.

A hulking giant with a bullet head and a barrel chest, the sergeant enjoyed his work and was a virtuoso at employing the various implements of his trade to inflict maximum suffering on his luckless victims. Dragunovic had pulled him out of a military mental hospital where he was serving a life sentence for a number of sadistic crimes.

Two of Radom's victims were now guests of the interrogation facilities. Dragunovic chain-lit another American filter cigarette as he stepped further inside and looked around.

The pungent tobacco smoke would help dispel some of the unpleasant odors that filled the chamber—odors of sweat, fear, blood, shit, piss and vomit—which Radom seemed to revel in but which Dragunovic, being more sane than the sergeant, would prefer to avoid.

Inhaling deeply, Dragunovic took in the grim tableau. It wasn't a pretty picture, but it was an expectable one.

Radom, stripped to the waist, his bare, muscular torso glistening with sweat, stood over a table on which one of the couriers was lashed facedown. Radom was holding an iron fireplace poker in one hand and a propane gas cylinder in the other, playing the yellow-blue flame across the tip of the poker, which by now glowed white-hot.

Radom looked at his superior as if for instructions and the colonel nodded. Even Dragunovic was prompted to look away as the sadist applied the poker to the helpless, naked man on the wooden slab. As he heard the victim's tormented screams, Dragunovic did not even want to contemplate what it must be like to experience such pain.

But the wretch on the table was not the object of the colonel's visit. Actually, his purpose was only to instruct the other courier in what awaited him if he were uncooperative. The other man hung twelve feet above the moist stone floor of the chamber, suspended by a rope lashed around his chest and under his arms.

The colonel crossed to a spot where he could look directly up at the suspended courier. He stood regarding the other's plight for a moment while he calmly smoked his cigarette, enjoying the taste of the tobacco.

"I hope you realize how fortunate you are, Janos," he told the naked man above him. "Radom might have strung you up by the wrists, in which case you would not be so comfortable as you are right now."

Dragunovic dragged again and exhaled creamy jets of smoke from his nostrils.

"Radom did that on my orders. You see, I wanted you to have every incentive to be cooperative. Your brother has suffered in your place. Do not make his sufferings to have been in vain. Tell me what I desire to know. I shall free you then. Both you and him."

The suspended man looked down but did not reply. Janos and his brother Imre had been couriers and bagmen for Dragunovic for the past year, making regular shuttle runs to points along the smuggling network that Dragunovic controlled from his mountain strongbase.

Dragunovic had expected them to be ready to depart at a moment's notice to wherever he sent them. Their missions took them to such distant places as Baghdad and Istanbul to the south, Greece and Albania to the west and Bulgaria and Romania to the north. They had ventured as far as Marseilles, France, on their commander's instructions.

During the course of their activities, the two Serb brothers had arranged for millions of dollars worth of weaponry, plunder, diamonds, drugs and other contraband to find its way from suppliers at one end of the smuggling chain to purchasers on the other. But the two couriers had gotten greedy and had begun doing side deals on their own.

Before long they had begun skimming regulary, transporting the goods to suppliers of their own, banking the proceeds in numbered offshore accounts. Dragunovic had begun suspecting something of the kind, but it wasn't actually their pilfering that had caused him to have them put to the lash.

It wasn't merely a matter of money. It was a matter of their having meddled in something beyond their understanding, of having lost—or stolen—an item that they had no right to even know about. It was the loss of that item that had gotten Dragunovic in trouble with those in Baghdad. He could not afford to get into such trouble again, he knew.

"One time more, Janos," Dragunovic asked the hanging man. "The item you were charged with delivering to my clients in Istanbul. What happened to it?"

Still the man said nothing.

"Would you prefer that Radom put the question to you?" Dragunovic asked. "He would, I am sure, be more than happy to do so. But you would then no longer be as comfortable as I have seen fit to make you." Dragunovic took another drag. "Again. What became of the item?"

This time the suspended man's lips trembled. He began to speak.

"I don't know what happened to it," he answered weakly. "We did nothing amiss. It was stolen from us by someone else."

"You know nothing of the term 'red clay,' then?"

Dragunovic asked. "It means nothing to you, then?"

"I have no idea what this means," the suspended man told him, coughing out the words. "I told you that."

"Think carefully. Are you certain of it? You are not lying, are you, Janos?"

"I tell you I do not know," the hanging man managed to rasp out again.

Dragunovic shook his head. He believed the courier. It would disappoint Radom to be deprived of his victims, at least for awhile, but Dragunovic wanted to think over what he had just learned. He ordered the two men removed from the interrogation chamber and placed in cells. An orderly, however, told the colonel that this was impossible.

"Why is that?"

"Because there are no more cells available, sir. They are all occupied," the soldier answered.

"That's not entirely true. A cell will soon be available," Dragunovic told the orderly. "Once you execute the former Colonel Danko in cell number two. Do so immediately."

The orderly nodded and saluted the commander. Dragunovic took a step forward then turned, as if he had just remembered something.

"Oh, yes," he told the soldier. "I had almost forgotten. Give the colonel a final cigarette before you shoot him. A good smoke will make him more relaxed—before he dies."

## chapter *six*

**A**fter the scattered elements of Cobra Force had
linked up at rally point Bravo, Saxon considered
whether or not to abort the mission.

On the one hand, the presence of the covert special
operations unit in the vicinity of the SAM belt had
surely been compromised. Yugo forces had engaged
them in combat, and while none had survived to be
debriefed, the regional commander could not fail to
draw the obvious conclusion. The Serb warlord who
controlled the military forces in the region would
have no reason to doubt that a U.S. or NATO special
forces team was operating in his domain.

Then again, the mountainous sector covered an
area of approximately 100 square miles. The forested
terrain was rugged, especially so in this late, cold
spring, and Dracula's garrison contained a limited

number of combat-worthy troops. Most of them were no doubt conscripts, and the majority of these had little or no field training or experience.

They were basically tenders for the handful of technicians overseeing surface-to-air missile launchers. Saxon judged that the Yugo warlord simply didn't have the resources to mount an effective live-fire reconnaissance mission against Cobra Force—not with the personnel he had available to him, anyway.

There was always the possibility that Dracula might arrange for better-trained personnel, possibly even Spetsnaz troops, to take over this duty. Cobra's mission was important enough for Saxon to take the risk—for the time being, anyway—of conducting operations while a peer-level force might be hunting his team.

The mobile SAM launchers under Dragunovic's control presented a formidable barrier to NATO air strikes against strategic targets in Bulgaria and Macedonia. Tomahawks and other cruise missiles, though effective, couldn't be used against *every* threat. There were just too many targets that could not be interdicted by any other means than a human pilot firing a missile or dropping a bomb at close range. It was Cobra's job to pave the way for coalition tacair forces to roll in and drop their loads on those targets.

Saxon called the team together and explained his decision to proceed with the mission. It turned out to be unanimous: All the Marines were good to go. The team then got down to the business of doing what they had been sent in to accomplish.

Although the F/A-18 fighter had been shot down,

the sortie had flown Macedonian airspace long enough to have accomplished its covert mission. The overflight had produced the intended results: The SAM search and tracking radars in this sector of the Yugo antiaircraft belt had been briefly turned on.

The RC-135 ferret that had been orbiting the region had been able to electronically fingerprint the SAM radars and match the sources of the pulse-Doppler signals they generated to points on a grid map. Those map coordinates were now programmed into the mobile Land Warrior computer units that were integrated into Cobra Force's combat gear.

Although the covert strike team could not depend on the mobile SAM launchers to be in the same places they had been at the time of the overflight, the data gave the team reliable points of reference so they could hunt down and kill the SAM sites.

Saxon and his team could be reasonably certain that the missile launchers could be located somewhere within a half-mile radius of their last known position; an average of the many sightings over the last few weeks had shown that while the units were highly mobile, the hide sites for the launchers were kept within a small area.

The individual SAM crews obviously had set up a system to prevent their units from bunching up. Keeping their launchers well-spaced would be essential not only for survivability, but also for effective radar coverage of the airspace.

Cobra Force had determined that a total of between six and eight mobile SAM sites were present in the vicinity. They would take out as many as possible and attempt to pinpoint the location of the remainder so that low altitude B-1B strikes could destroy those that remained in place.

Saxon decided that the team would operate in the mountains for as long as it was able to function effectively. As soon as the operation reached the point of diminishing returns, he would order up a heliborne extraction for the team.

But that was at least days away. Right now, the team had its work cut out for it.

T he Mi-8 HIP transport chopper flared and its nose wheels touched down onto the dusty earth of the windswept mountain battlefield.

Twelve men in woodland camouflage BDUs emerged from the rear clamshell doors of the Soviet helicraft, holding their soft-brimmed bush hats down against the propwash of the HIP's dishing rotorblades with one hand and gripping their folding stock–equipped AKS-74 assault rifles in the other.

After jumping from the helo to the ground, they loped on shallow crouches across the barren vale, their eyes alert, their weapons tracking.

The first man out of the chopper was Master Sergeant Yuri Batalin, commander of the Spetsnaz unit, who had been ordered to chase down and kill the unfriendly patrol now known to be operating in the vicinity.

The remainder of the men were made up of sergeants and corporals; few if any Spetsnaz teams were comprised of ranks higher than sergeant or lower than private first-class, and this team was no exception. Batalin was the ranking NCO in the unit, but the men accepted his leadership because they recognized that he excelled them all in combat experience, professionalism, iron nerve and raw courage.

Before setting out to exterminate the American special forces unit in the sector—in his mind they were already American rather than British SAS or some sort of NATO formation, because only the Americans possessed any credible anti-SAM forces— Batalin had ordered his team flown to the site of the battle between the unfriendlies and Yugo regulars.

He wanted to inspect the site to determine what he could about the composition and tactics of the enemy. Like a bloodhound, he wanted to fill his nose with the scent of his quarry. Then he could track them to the ends of the earth if need be.

The corpses still littered the battlefield, lying where they had fallen on the frigid, sparsely tufted earth. The unseasonably bitter cold had preserved the casualties, yet nothing could prevent the scent of death from insinuating itself into the air. A veteran of many battlefields, Batalin recognized the familiar rankness, despite the meat-locker conditions on the plateau.

Batalin at once detected the unmistakable signs of a skillful heliborne extraction of the pilot under heavy fire.

The Yugo regulars had been pugnacious but inept. They had charged the American commando forces head-on, apparent from the positions and postures of the fallen. Yet the Americans had enjoyed assistance from the crew of the helicopter.

The pockmarks of heavy machine-gun rounds and the shell casings of 7.62mm bullets among the brass ejected by smaller caliber weapons were everywhere. They gave testament to the immense firepower that had been leveled against the Yugo patrol and had turned their own makeshift ambush against them in the end.

Batalin rose from his crouched position, jingling a mixture of three types of shell casings in the hollow of his combat-gloved right hand. He walked on through the battlefield, his mind conjuring up the sounds of gunfire, the shouts of the combatants, the tortured cries of the dying.

The Spetsnaz stepped toward the tree line at the edge of the clearing, his trained senses searching for signs of the American presence. Here and there Batalin found clusters of spent brass, giving testament to where the commando forces had been positioned during the firefight.

As he built up his mental reconstruction of events, Batalin nodded to himself in affirmation of his suspicions. The enemy unit could not have been more than a small one, perhaps no more than three or four men.

Perhaps there were others at a remote location or observation post—at this thought Batalin shaded his eyes and gazed into the sunlight toward a nearby ridgeline—but the forces engaged in the firefight could not have been more than a squad.

Their commander had shown imagination and discretion in positioning his troops for maximum lethality. He had also shown his acumen in extracting from the site, for he had covered his tracks well. Still, there would be some indication of the direction he had taken.

"Zumetkin! Morozov!" Batalin called two of his men toward him.

The two commandos loped quickly from the other side of the vale toward where their leader stood. Reaching him, they stood at crisp attention.

"Yes, sir," they said, practically in unison.

"Stand at ease," Batalin ordered, his cold grey eyes playing across the hard faces of the two veteran soldiers like a laser gun. "You have had the opportunity to look over the area?"

"Yes, sir."

"What have you to report? Zumetkin, you first."

"Sir, the battlefield shows the signs of intense automatic weapons fire. Intense but brief from the nature of the way the Yugo regulars seem to have been killed. The battle could not have lasted long, but it must have been quite a nasty one while it went on."

Batalin nodded.

"You, Morozov, what have you to add?"

"Sir," the wiry corporal began, his eyes unflinchingly bearing the scrutiny of his commander's icy stare. "These must have been commando forces of superb training and courage," he declared. "I have no doubt that although they benefited from the helo support, they would have destroyed the ambush force quite effectively on their own, well before reinforcements could have arrived at this remote location."

"Very good," Batalin acknowledged. "Here is what I wish for you to do next. Gather the rest of the troop.

Comb the perimeter for signs of an exit corridor. I desire to know in which direction the enemy commandos extracted from the firefight."

"Yes, sir," Batalin's men both said, then saluted and left to carry out their orders. Batalin watched as his troopers fanned out along the periphery of the battlezone. A short time later, he saw a red signal flare in the distance. It had been fired by Morozov.

"Here, Commander." The voice of the sergeant came over the comms unit. "There are signs of extraction on this slope."

Batalin looked outward, drawing an imaginary line to the series of forested ridgelines to the southeast of their position. A grim smile crossed his jagged features.

"Yes," he said. "The Plakenska Planina—Plakenska Mountain. I would go there too."

Their quarry was somewhere in those distant hills. The hunt was on.

Cobra Force, once again a unit at full strength, had humped through the night. The force reached the coordinates of its first target shortly before daybreak and began to reconnoiter.

As the dawn came, Cobra got lucky. The clanking of tank treads, the whining of pneumatic pistons, the roar of diesel engines and the gripes and curses of men pitting themselves against balky machines and biting cold echoed through the woods.

The telltale sounds were unmistakable. One of the mobile SAM units was being moved from cover ei-

ther for antiaircraft duty in anticipation of further
NATO strike packages passing overhead, or for regular maintenance of the launcher and missiles and
calibration of the tracking radars.

Saxon tasked Hirsh and Mooner with the reconnaissance duty. They were to determine the precise
location of the mobile SAM crew, which usually
numbered no more than five men, and report back via
radio.

Once the location was known, the rest of the commando force would attack the outpost, killing all personnel before a radio alert could be sent and then
blowing up the missiles, launcher vehicle and mobile
radar installation. The force would then extract from
the area.

After a short time, the recon party made contact
with Saxon via communications link. To preserve security, wrist-top keypads were used to tap out wireless E-mail messages over the communications net.
No talk would give away the party's position.

*Found the SAM site*, the message scrolled across
Saxon's ITD eyephone in real time.

Hirsh gave the reconnaissance party's position on
a grid map of the area. Saxon ordered the men with
him to move out and link up with Hirsh and Mooner.

Once the teams united, Cobra would conduct a final reconnoiter and then proceed with its mission.
The SAM site was to be destroyed. Its crew and all
support personnel were to be wiped out. There would
be no enemy prisoners.

# chapter *seven*

**T**he SA-10 "Grumble" missile launch system, as versatile a piece of military hardware as it is lethal—and as complex as it is both—is made up of two main components. The first is the mobile launcher, a heavy GAZ truck bed on which up to four SAM launch canisters containing the 48N6 surface-to-air missiles are mounted. An SA-10 battery may be made up of one or multiple launch vehicles.

The system's second component is the search, tracking and fire-control radar. The radar panel and other antennae are also mounted on a modified truck bed and tended by a three-man crew. In a typical SA-10 mobile installation a security detail may also be present to provide limited fire support.

The maintenance functions for the system need to be carried out in the open because, among other reasons, the radars need to be briefly turned on in test mode.

On this cold morning, the muted sounds of activity echoing through the woods signaled that just such maintenance operations were being carried out. The Marine force watched through binoculars as the launch vehicle and mobile radar unit lumbered along a narrow dirt road that snaked through stands of fir, pine and other hardy mountain trees.

Hirsh and Mooner, Cobra Force's reconnaissance party, had spotted the SAM crew about an hour before. The bulky mobile launcher had been camouflaged in a wooded thicket, its chassis painted in a woodland camo pattern.

The four 48N6 missiles that the squat, tracked launch vehicle carried like some prehistoric creature with exposed fangs were draped completely in camouflage netting. Both missiles and launch vehicle were further concealed under a dense, leafy covering of tree branch cuttings.

But sounds and movement had given away the position of the launcher. Security measures were extremely lax. The mobile SAM crew might have posted pickets on the perimeter, but it hadn't, so the Marine reconnaissance element had been able to get up fairly close to the launcher's hide site and observe Hugo without being detected.

First a detail of the SAM crew pulled off the branches and clusters of leaves that had draped the launcher, tossing the cut foliage to the ground around the tracked chassis. The camouflage netting around the missiles themselves continued to be left in place.

While this activity went on, the launch crew climbed inside the APC-like vehicle to power up the electronic systems and boot up the onboard computers. As these two details performed their duties, the driver started the mobile launcher's engine and warmed it, letting it idle. The remainder of the crew, Yugo regulars armed with AK-47s and an RPK light machine gun, stood around checking their weapons and sharing a smoke.

In just under a half hour these preparations were completed and the SAM launcher vehicles rolled out of the hide site and onto the narrow mountain track. From here the mobile SAMs passed onto a tertiary road that snaked along a series of forested ridgelines. Hirsh and Mooner considered taking out the vehicles then and there—the radar truck and missiles would go crashing down into the gorge below—but they were under-strength for the mission.

Saxon concurred with this decision when the two-man team reported in. The Cobra Force commander gave his field people a rally point along the projected path of the launch detail's advance.

Hirsh and Mooner were to double-time it to this point across rugged terrain. The idea was to arrive ahead of the Yugos. When the reconnaissance detail hooked up with the main team element, a moving ambush would already be set up for the mobile SAM crew.

Saxon picked a site around an elbow in the narrow lane to set up an L-shaped ambush. The site was ideally suited to his plans: The road was bordered on one side by high ground with shrubs and rocks for cover; on the other side was a sheer drop of about 300 feet, straight down into a steep gorge with a narrow river at its bottom.

Saxon placed half of the team on the far side of the elbow and the other half on the near side, less himself and two other Marines who would straddle the bend on the heights and act as lookouts.

Positioned on the high ground behind cover, Saxon enjoyed a bird's-eye view of the approach to the ambush point. He unshipped a pair of digitally enhanced binoculars and scanned the undulating mountain road. The binoculars were laser-augmented and automatically focused on the mobile TEL approaching from a wooded stretch in the distance.

The binoculars also calculated the distance between the launcher vehicles and the ambush point. A dim blue numerical readout told Saxon that the target was one-point-five klicks away and counting down. Saxon shipped away the binocs as position reports from the two fire teams on either side of the L came in over SINCGARS radio commlink.

"Team One in position," Chicken Wire reported. "One bloodthirsty Pig and two SMAWs ready to party."

Down on the near side bend of the L, Chicken Wire and two others behind the Marine version of the Army's light antitank weapon launchers were hunkered down at the base of the hill.

Separated at twenty-foot intervals, the Marines formed a gauntlet of steel and explosives through which the unfriendly force would have to pass. In the unlikely event that the enemy survived running the gauntlet, the reserves placed on the far end of the bend would mop up any stragglers with more shoulder-launched multipurpose assault weapons.

"Team Two in position," the second ambush crew reported.

Saxon took up the binoculars again. The mobile TEL had continued its slow advance along the road. Then, surprisingly, it suddenly halted.

Saxon watched in growing anticipation as two Yugo troopers riding on top of the SAM vehicle jumped off and began to walk back and gesture at the driver, directing the ponderous trucks up close against the side of a nearby hillside.

A few minutes later the parking operation was completed. The crew of the TEL emerged and began putting out orange road marker cones every six feet or so. When this was completed, they lit two hazard flares and tossed one about fifty yards in front of the TEL and the other the same distance behind it.

Saxon keyed his comms and reported the change in situation to the force elements deployed in brackets around the ambush site.

"The TEL convoy has stopped moving," he reported. "It appears to have been deliberately parked half a kilometer up the road. Hold your positions."

"What's wrong?" Mooner asked from his position leading the second fire team. "They got mechanical trouble, you think?"

"Negative. There's no sign of mechanical failure I

can see. This is either a planned stop or they've been ordered to stop by command."

"Maybe they're waiting for something," Hirsh put in over the unit's communications net.

"Maybe."

"But for what?"

"That's the money question," Saxon said. "We'll have to see." Saxon turned behind him. "Jekyll, can we get Improved Crystal coverage on the area?"

"I'll try, sir," Jekyll reported. "Cloud cover might be a problem, though."

Saxon already knew about that. The weather had turned bad on them within the last few hours and a cold drizzle had begun to fall.

"Do what you can," Saxon ordered.

"Good to go, sir," Jekyll answered.

A few minutes later Jekyll had logged on to the Kennan-class PHOTINT satellite parked in geosynchronous low earth orbit above the southern Balkans, its telemetry available to Cobra Force for real-time field analysis. The portable ground station unit was shockproof and weatherproof.

"Sir, the imagery is not conclusive due to heavy cloud cover but there does appear to be a large force of heavy vehicles moving toward our position along the road below. I figure it as a mechanized column. Tanks and APCs."

"How big?"

"Not very," Jekyll reported. "Company strength, maybe." He added, "Tubes are not facing away, repeat, not facing away."

Sgt. Wayne Riggs, Saxon's XO, crouched to the team leader's left.

"What the hell do you think we got here, boss?" he asked. "You think they made us?"

"I don't know if it's a threat or not," Saxon answered, thinking that just because tank cannons were positioned forward didn't mean they were on alert. Saxon got on commo and passed the word to the ambush teams on the bend to stay in position until he ordered otherwise.

The minutes ticked off. The TEL crew still remained in position. Saxon watched them through worsening rain.

They did not appear nervous or agitated in any way; they simply appeared bored. Some of the soldiers smoked while others moved around. They looked like men with time on their hands.

One soldier threw rocks over the side of the cliff and into the gorge below. Had there been an alert they would not act this nonchalantly, Saxon reasoned. He became convinced that whatever was coming, it had nothing to do with Cobra's presence.

Still, the tension mounted as the mechanized force drew nearer. They could now hear the rumbling and clanking of the many vehicles, could already smell the acrid stench of diesel exhaust blown their way on the rain-moistened wind.

The Marines stood pat as the force came into more direct view. Saxon continued to man the binoculars as the tank column broached the first warning flare and slowed to creep past the conical road markers. As the big vehicles passed, some of their crew waved at the men standing around the missile launcher, and one soldier tossed a pack of cigarettes their way.

The tension ebbed from Saxon's frame as the column swept past the ambush point, taking no notice of the Marine force deployed in sparse cover only a few feet away from its flank.

Those Marines closest to the passing tanks and armored personnel carriers were pelted with small rocks and road debris thrown off by the big tires and tank treads and had to hold their breath against noxious exhaust fumes. Mooner suffered most ignobly of all as a Yugo trooper standing atop a slow-moving APC launched a stream of urine all over him.

Some fifteen minutes later, the mechanized column had rolled past the Marines' ambush position. But Saxon knew that the ambush might have to be scrubbed if the TEL detail moved away too slowly. If Cobra Force moved too fast, the armor that had just passed by would still be in hearing range of the sounds of automatic fire and high-explosive and radio for more mobile forces to come in to investigate.

Saxon kept his eyes glued on the TEL crew. Minutes had already passed and by now the last rumble of the armored column had completely died away, but still the SAM crew remained where it had parked, seemingly in no hurry to leave.

Saxon wondered if there was something else coming up the road but Jekyll saw nothing from overhead surveillance to indicate this. Saxon continued to watch the TEL crew. He surmised that they were simply in no hurry to get going, probably because they wanted to give the armor lurching up the road ahead a sizable lead in order to avoid having to call another halt.

Whatever the reason for the delay, the SAM crew continued to linger at its position for another quarter hour. Then it slowly got going again. Men started up the engines and the launcher vehicles commenced rolling down the road again.

Saxon keyed his comms and ordered Teams One and Two to prepare to hit the TEL convoy when it came into position. The minutes ticked off and the Marines tensed for battle. This was a go. It was going to turn bad and bloody soon and every member of the team knew it.

"Roadrunner! Roadrunner!" Saxon said into his comms. It was the prearranged signal to open up on the TEL.

Chicken Wire's Pig suddenly began to chatter. The dull, hammering thuds of 7.62mm NATO standard rounds announced the commencement of the ambush. From his vantage point Saxon saw the devastating result of the M60's sustained fire.

The armor-piercing rounds raked across the flanks of the first of the lumbering vehicles, pocking steel plate and chewing up two Yugo regulars riding up top of the radar truck. The men were killed instantly, bloody chunks of meat and bone matter spraying from the corpses before they fell to the ground.

Before the driver could stop the truck, two Marines, Loggins and Ramirez, fired 83mm SMAW rounds into the cab, directly through its windows. At

medium range the antiarmor rocket strikes were lethal.

The men riding inside the cab were killed instantly.
The GAZ rolled to a slow stop. It began to burn,
flames licking from the underside and from the interior behind the cab. Dense black smoke twisted into
the air like a rope ladder from hell.

Saxon waited a minute and decided that the soldiers inside the troop carriage compartment of the
TEL vehicle had been killed in the rocket assault
along with the driver. Nobody could survive more
than a few seconds in the heat and toxic smoke of
the strike.

Another strike had crippled the launch vehicle. The
camouflage netting that shrouded the missiles had
also begun to burn. Saxon knew that within a very
short time either their liquid fuel or their warheads
would ignite and explode. He judged the fuel would
ignite first because it was far more volatile than the
explosives in the warheads.

Saxon gave instructions for the team to move out
of the ambush site along the predetermined line of
withdrawal, which was back onto the high ground
and into the woods. Once they reached their hide site
he would decide whether or not to call for a helo
extraction. Apart from any other consideration, the
worsening weather picture might scrub the rest of the
mission.

Spetsnaz NCO Yuri Batalin had followed the projected line of withdrawal from the high mountain

vale. A heliborne funeral detail would gather up the Yugo soldiers' bodies and bring them back to Split for military burial.

He and his men had seen enough and were now on the trail of their elusive quarry. But the worsening weather situation was slowing them, limiting mobility and visibility both on the ground and in the sky. Batalin stared out through the helo's open side hatch at the wet mess outside.

A cold rain, mixed with sleet, was falling and a dense blanket of fog had rolled down from the mountaintops into hollow places on the land below. There was no more use in going on too much longer. Batalin knew he would have to turn back to base and venture out again when the weather cleared.

He was just about to signal to his troops on the ground to form up for helo extraction and return to base when the pilot informed Batalin that he was wanted on the radio.

The Spetsnaz commander took the handset and learned that a mobile launcher had just blown up several kilometers distant from their current position. A mechanized force was being dispatched to the area to reconnoiter and file a damage report. Batalin asked to be kept informed of any suspicious occurrences that might indicate enemy sabotage, which could indicate the presence of those he hunted.

Batalin handed back the handset and issued instructions to the pilot: Set down and pick up the remainder of the team on the ground, then proceed to base by way of the position of the reported explosion. His quarry had struck. He was sure of this.

Batalin suspected that the TEL had met its fate in an ambush. If nothing else, he wanted to overfly the area to have a look before they returned to garrison headquarters near the regional capital, Gostivar.

The Spetsnaz commander issued his orders to the pilot and began making his way from the cockpit toward the crew compartment at the aircraft's rear.

At that moment he heard the pilot shout with surprise and panic.

Turning around, he saw something huge and black loom precipitously up out of the enshrouding blanket of dense mist. A moment later it was as if the chopper had slammed straight into a massive brick wall. Batalin was thrown to the deck by the force of impact, breaking his nose. As the pain seared through his injured face, he felt the helo lurch sideways and knew that they were falling.

# chapter *eight*

**T**he ground fog was dense as cotton wadding, and kept spraying them with millions of freezing droplets of rain. Marine Force One was humping its way through a cloud in extremely poor visibility conditions. They were navigating more like fighter pilots than mud Marines.

The colored, moving-map overlays in their eyephones allowed them to navigate the land by GPS. The icons on their map displays showed the direction the team was to march to its next waypoint. Thanks to the technology, what would have been slow and dangerous going was speeded up and simplified.

Distant thunder pealed and boomed, echoing from peak to peak, from ridge to ridge, from valley to valley. The sky was lit from time to time by flashes of lightning that strangely strobed and flickered through the dense blanket of swirling fog. The team pushed on, eager to get out of the weather and bunker in against the oncoming night.

Interspersed amid the sounds of nature, sometimes fainter, sometimes louder depending on the way the sound echoed through the mountains, the team also heard another sound.

A man-made sound. One they all recognized.

It was the sound of a jet-assisted helicopter, the scream of ramjet turbines and the coffee-grinder chugging of dishing rotorblades unmistakable in the distance.

Like the rest of the unit, Saxon had been listening to the sound for some minutes. He knew it was a helo, but not a friendly one, from the sound it made. He judged that the chopper was probably on a routine flight, however, and ordered the team to pay no attention to it unless the situation changed. Unless it was a sound made by a circling, hunting aircraft, for example.

The team continued to press onward through the fog. Lightning flashed again, and almost immediately a thunderous double-boom sounded in the distance. Saxon stopped and listened, as did the rest of the team. Moments later the true thunder sounded, the sharp, ripping cracks audibly different from the duller booms they had heard before.

That first sound had been no thunderclap, all now knew. But it hadn't been artillery fire either. What was it?

Another explosion suddenly ripped, rolled and ech-oed over the hills and valleys, this one clearly produced by man-made combustibles. Almost simultaneously they heard the clamor of men shouting. No way that was artillery.

Saxon said, "That's got to be the helo. Must have hit something in the fog."

His mind flashed back to a Marine operation five years before, in the African republic of Zambia. He had been onboard a Marine Sea Stallion lifting off with a collection of refugees. There had been a heavy fog condition then too. The helo pilot had almost hit an overhead electrical cable, one of the high ones strung on steel towers, righting the aircraft at the last moment.

The recollection sparked a thought. Saxon keyed his map display system, searching for high-voltage wire towers in the vicinity. In a second or two his hunch was confirmed. There was a line of high-tension cables running up a fire gap in the mountains on a north-northeast vector. The chopper had probably hit the cables and gotten its rotors tangled. After that, it could have smashed into one of the steel pylons supporting the cables.

Saxon studied the map display a moment longer. It might be best to move on toward the team's hide site. On the other hand, Saxon's combat instincts were telling him something about the chopper.

He wondered who had been onboard and what it contained, and if anything of tactical value might be salvaged from the wreckage. If some of those onboard were still alive they might be interrogated. Only a small detour from the team's line of march would be necessary to reconnoiter. Saxon decided to act on his hunch.

"Pass the word," he told his XO. "We're gonna check out what happened to that chopper."

F or a moment Batalin did not know where he was. He had been floating in a realm of hellish darkness, a black, oily subterranean pool broken by lights and horrible noises. It had been the end of the world.

Then he had suddenly come back to his senses. The fuzzy half-awareness broke open like an egg and he emerged into the real world, his mind immediately snapping into sharp, crisp focus.

The Spetsnaz leader came to lying on his back. He smelled the charred odor of flesh seared by semi-molten, cooked-off shrapnel—his own, perhaps?—and saw the smoldering wreckage all about him. To one side, the hulk of the fallen Hip transport helo lay like the carcass of a prehistoric sauropod.

Flickering tongues of scorching flame licked upward from the depths of the shattered wreckage and toxic sheets of noxious smoke boiled out of the burning interior of the helo to mingle with the still-heavy fog that had caused the crash in the first place.

Batalin rose to his feet, staggered for a moment, then regained control of his bruised limbs. Blood from his shattered nose streamed down his face, already congealing. Grateful that nothing else had been broken in the crash, he ran his gaze along the trunk of the downed helicraft to the mangled remains of the cockpit, where his guess at the cause of the crash was confirmed.

Sparking electrical cables lay on the ground; one immense steel support pylon had been sawed almost completely in half. The tapered upper end listed at an angle nearly perpendicular to its intact base.

Suverov, Batalin's XO, came running toward him. His fatigues were smudged with soot and stained with smoke, his face blistered, his hair singed.

"Sir. Thank goodness you are alive."

"Never mind me. What about the troop?"

"We have four men confirmed dead and five wounded, two of them severely. I and Sergeant Rudenko were lucky. We were thrown clear during the crash and are unhurt."

"And the cockpit crew?"

Suverov shook his head.

"Both dead, sir, I'm afraid."

"Have you radioed for assistance?"

"There is no radio. The helo's communications were damaged and our own have been lost."

"Lost? How in hell were they lost?"

"Many things were spilled from the wreckage. It was like a matchbox full of insects being shaken by a giant. I have detailed Kopolev and Barsov to search for the radio, however."

Batalin clapped his XO on the shoulder.

"I am sorry, Fedor," he apologized. "Good work. Carry on."

"You should be looked at, sir," Suverov said. "I will send for the medic."

"There's no need," Batalin told him. "I'm all right. Have him see to the others first."

Suverov saluted and loped off toward the other side of the wrecked hulk lying in the snow.

Batalin cursed. Of all the damned luck! Then he realized he had lost his rifle. He would have to search for it.

Cobra Force halted its march and conducted a fast recon of the crash site. The detour proved to be a short one. As the Marines proceeded forward, the smell of smoke and the shouting of men in distress acted as beacons to guide them through the dense fog.

Within an hour, they had drawn abreast of the downed chopper's position. The Marines moved silently through the forest and reached a place of concealment and vantage without being detected by the victims of the crash.

They had been alert for lookouts placed on the perimeter, but had found no sign of any sentries. Saxon suspected that the survivors of the crash were still in a state of near-shock, tending to their wounded and trying to contact rescue personnel.

From behind a thin line of tall trees, Saxon and Da Noiz peered through binoculars at the crash site. As Saxon had suspected, a helicopter had gone down. From its markings and camouflage-pattern paint job Saxon determined it to be a Soviet Hip flown by the Yugoslavian air force. Further scrutiny revealed the passengers onboard the helo as either Yugoslavian or Russian special forces troops. Apart from the floppy-brimmed campaign hats they wore, which were not standard issue for Yugo regular forces, their BDUs bore the clearly recognizable shield-on-dagger unit patch of elite Spetsnaz specialist troops.

Saxon counted a number of dead arranged on the near side of the wreckage. There were also apparently many wounded among the survivors.

All told, the contingent was of approximately platoon strength. Saxon swept the binoculars across the crash site and noted one of the Spetsnaz bore master sergeant's stripes.

He was certain that this was the ranking officer of the troop. He watched as the platoon commander gave orders to his subordinate, was saluted and began searching for something amid the wreckage.

Saxon put down the field glasses and reflected a moment on what he had just witnessed. The Spetsnaz contingent might have been en route to some other destination, but he doubted this. The region was fairly remote and was not a likely air corridor used to shuttle troops to regional Yugo garrisons.

On the other hand, there was the possibility that had suggested itself to Saxon when he'd first heard the helo: that the Spetsnaz formation had been engaged in a reconnaissance by fire mission against a hostile target—Cobra Force itself. The conviction that the Spetsnaz had been sent out to hunt down and kill Saxon and his team now became an inescapable conclusion.

"What do we do about 'em?" asked Da Noiz.

Saxon had decided that too.

"Absolutely nothing," he said. "Taking them out has no direct bearing on our mission and we've gained a valuable piece of intelligence in spotting them before they might have spotted us. They look like they might be out of action for some time. I think we'll just bypass them."

Saxon picked up the binocs and took another look. At that moment, a frightened hare darted from the tree line into the clearing beyond beneath the high-tension cables.

The brown streak of motion was caught by Corporal Mironovskiy as he cleaned his AK-47, which he had custom-fitted with a telescopic sight. Mironovskiy smiled as he saw the rabbit run. Things had not gone entirely wrong—they would have some fresh meat tonight to complement their rations should they have to spend the night in this hell-stricken place.

Mironovskiy was an excellent shot and knew he could easily bag the hare. He lifted his rifle to shoulder height and sighted on the rabbit. The hare was pinned at the circle at the center of the crossed blue reticle lines, but Mironovskiy held his fire. What he saw framed in the upper left quadrant of the viewfield made his breath catch in his lungs.

Soldiers in NATO woodland camouflage—and they were watching him and the rest of the troop.

"Enemy soldiers!" Mironovskiy shouted and, without waiting for instructions, immediately began firing into the trees.

It would prove to be a rash move and a very costly mistake for the Spetsnaz.

\*     \*     \*

**B**atalin's head snapped toward the right at the sound of Mironovskiy's shouted warning, then quickly snapped into line with the direction the rifle was pointing. Time slowed to a crawl even as his mind calculated at a speed beyond the capacity of word-based thought.

He too now saw what he had missed before: the glimpses of camouflage patterning amid the mottled arrangement of natural foliage, tree bark, earth and rock.

It was the supreme irony, he knew. Here were the very American commandos that his Spetsnaz had been ordered to hunt down and kill. There was no doubt in his mind that this was so. No doubt whatsoever.

Due to a twist of fate, they—not his troop—were now in a position to exterminate the other. Batalin knew what would happen next with an inevitable certainty.

Yet even as he began to shout "Hold fire!" Mironovskiy had opened up with a three-round automatic burst. Before Batalin could say or do anything else, other members of the Spetsnaz were shooting without discipline into the tree line, disoriented and frightened men reacting without thinking.

It all happened quickly and with lethal progression after that. Answering fire erupted from the tree line. Muzzle flashes from a row of automatic weapons spaced at intervals highlighted the positions of the otherwise concealed troops behind the fringe of forest vegetation.

The metallic chattering of blowback-driven bolt actions rose to a crescendo as Batalin dropped to his belly and opened up with the AKS-74 he had just pulled from beneath the thin, crusty layer of ice and impacted snow. Like it or not, the troop was now committed to the firefight. There was no turning back. They were locked in combat with the enemy.

**S**axon had no choice either. Response was driven by the force of events, not tactics. He had ordered the squad to fire back at the Spetsnaz. The mission had abruptly changed from pure reconnaissance to a recon by fire.

Cobra's presence in the area had been confirmed by the Spetsnaz commando force at the wreckage site. With this information known to the enemy, their lives as well as their mission were compromised. No prisoners were to be taken. The Yugo special forces would die heroes' deaths. But they would be just as dead in the end as any coward.

The dull staccato of Chicken Wire's M60 machine gun formed a low basso counterpoint to the higher-pitched chattering of the Commando assault weapons as the Marines engaged the hostile forces. Three Marines armed with SMAWs were setting up to fire the man-portable launchers' armor-piercing warheads into the enemy fire position.

Saxon had given the SMAW squad orders to aim into the center of the enemy position and open up as soon as they had a target in their sights.

It was not long before the first rocket streaked from

its shoulder-mounted firing tube on a low, straight arc into the clearing beyond.

As it exploded near the hulk of the helo, the second and third SMAW rockets were unleashed on the enemy force.

The combined rocket strikes caused a deafening multiple explosion and threw up gouts of smoke and pulverized earth, for a moment obscuring the impact zone from the Marines' eyes. Secondary explosions from the helo's fuel tanks and weapons stores cooked off now too, and pinwheels of many-colored sparks went spraying high into the air and whizzing off like Roman candles into the tree line.

When the smoke of battle finally cleared and the explosions subsided, nothing lived but the flames that licked afresh at the wreckage. Bodies of fallen enemy littered the crash site. None of the downed men showed any sign of life. Saxon gave orders for his troop to pitch grenades into the carnage for insurance. He wanted to make absolutely certain that all enemy troops were dead.

# chapter *nine*

The straits that divided the southern Adriatic from the Ionian Seas were choppy and gray beneath the low-scudding underbelly of the V-22. The Osprey flew a due west course heading for the Italian coast and passed the port city of San Cataldo. It then banked and swept south toward the USFORCECOM operational command center at Otranto.

The Osprey was returning from a dangerous and remote LZ in Macedonia, where it had extracted Cobra Force personnel in response to Saxon's radioed request to HQ.

Helped, in some part, by the bad weather that had enveloped the mountains, the unit had staged a second successful assault on a Yugo surface-to-air missile installation. But by then, nearly forty-eight hours following the firefight, the troop was exhausted and suffering from exposure to the cold.

Added to the security threat posed by the presence of Spetsnaz troops in the vicinity, and the increased alert status of SAM units now that Cobra Force had destroyed a second mobile missile battery, Saxon judged that the team had overstayed its welcome.

Moreover, the weather pattern had worsened. A severe winter storm—the Navy meteorologists insisted on calling it a "winter storm" although it was late April already—was expected, and operations would have to be canceled until the weather picture changed for the better.

The Osprey crew had only a matter of hours in which to transit Macedonia and pick up the team before the weather picture altered radically. If the airborne rescue mission was too slow or if it hit any serious snags, it could become caught in a blinding whiteout and easily crash.

The blizzard had worsened considerably on the crossing of Albania, and the pilot had considered setting down until the storm cleared. But then he had broken through into better weather; as the Osprey began the Adriatic crossing, the snow had tapered off into a steady rain, but visibility was fair enough for the journey to proceed unhindered.

Saxon used the downtime of the trip back to Otranto to reflect on the team's two antimissile strikes and compare them. There would be after-action reports to file, not to mention a classified debriefing with the CIA present.

Saxon wanted to be on his toes. Cobra Force was

a new concept and, to many of his superiors, an un-
proven one. He always felt on the defensive during
debriefings, could never tell precisely who was a
friend of Cobra Force and who was a foe. Saxon
knew one thing for sure, and that was that Cobra was
seen as competition by other special forces branches.

The Navy SEALs especially had it in for the Marines' bid to enter the uncharted regions of special
forces personnel. Saxon recalled only too well how
bitterly the Navy brass had fought against the concept
of a Marine special operations unit that might rival
its own and steal its thunder and glory.

To many it had been blasphemy to endow the Marines with such an SF capability. This catechism was
echoed by Marine officers who claimed that the
Corps already was an elite unit and didn't need any
hot-shit special ops snake eaters to muck things up.
It was only because of the president's direct support
that the force had come into being at all. Had the
White House not blessed it, Cobra would have died
stillborn.

Because of the controversy surrounding Cobra
Force, the team needed to work harder than any other
special forces units just to justify their existence in
the special forces pantheon. One slipup and the bureaucrats and the time-servers and the SF-haters and
the SEAL commanders who were Cobra Force's
archenemies would see to it that the elite unit was
disbanded.

Saxon wasn't about to let that happen. He made
sure his people were the boldest and the baddest. He
worked them constantly, pushed them hard and ex-

pected them to always be ready and in peak performance mode. Few let him down, fewer washed out of Cobra's rigorous training program.

Now, even the SEALs who had laughed at Saxon's methods were sniffing around Cobra Force's dedicated training center and compound at Camp Lejeune, North Carolina, trying to match some of Saxon's innovations to their own training and recruitment programs.

Apart from having to have his shit together when he met with the brass and the Company spooks at Otranto, Saxon also wanted to make mental notes of the strong and weak points of the mission. These would prove vital in future training scenarios for the force, which Saxon was continuously improving and toughening.

He thought back to the team's last strike on the second SAM launch site.

Cobra had come upon the SAM crew setting up in the early morning hours. The missile battery was fully operational and its radars were turned on, evident from the movement of their dishes sweeping the sky for NATO military aircraft.

Saxon had given orders for the team to surround the installation and open up on it with small arms fire and the last of their supply of SMAW rockets. The concentrated salvos of bullets and high explosives had destroyed the transporter-erector-launcher system in place.

Still, the SA-10 missiles themselves had survived the strike, and so Saxon had dispatched Mooner and Frazzini to wire C-4 charges to the launch vehicle and set the charges for delayed detonation. He also ordered that two blocks of C-4 be rigged as booby traps in case any troops reached the strike zone before the charges blew. Concealed trip wires connected to chemical initiators would detonate the C-4.

From a distance Cobra watched a motorized contingent of Yugo troops rush up on an access road. The deuce-and-a-half contained a platoon of Yugo regulars who jumped off the truck at the hectoring of their sergeant and began combing the area. They were in almost perfect proximity to the center of the blast zone when one of the Yugos stepped across the near-invisible nylon trip wire and detonated one of the booby traps.

The C-4 charges blew and ignited the high-explosive warheads of the four SA-10 missiles. A miniature firestorm erupted from the combined blasts. All of the Yugos were killed almost instantaneously. Those closest to the missiles were virtually disintegrated by the intense heat and concussion of the strike.

Those a little further out were literally torn limb from limb, their bodies ripped to shreds by the severe blast and flying, jagged, semimolten pieces of shrapnel that cooked out of the exploding warheads.

Those on the outskirts of the blast zone were mortally wounded by the massive amounts of shrapnel thrown off by the detonation of the missile warheads. A smoking blast crater was gouged at the center of the SAM battery. That was all that was left to tell the tale.

\*    \*    \*

The Osprey soon reached its destination, flared above the marked stretch of runway and set down on its landing gear.

There were lessons to be learned from what had gone down on the strike, and Saxon filed them away in his memory bank. Though back behind friendly lines, he knew he couldn't relax a minute. He would soon be on the grill.

The Marine headquarters at Otranto was part of USFORCECOM, the American complement of the NATO coalition in the Balkans. Otranto's function was as a convenient staging and support base for fighter sorties and bomber missions into the strike areas in Macedonia and Bulgaria where Soviet and Bulgarian communist forces were operating.

Otranto was an ideal base for the Marines because it gave them fast and direct access to the southern Albanian coastline by surface vessel. From the Italian coastal city, Marine aviation also had access to a direct air corridor into the interior of the southern Balkans.

Otranto was also the location for the Marine hospital severe combat injuries unit, the main headquarters for the CIA, a location for soldiers on leave from the fighting and headquarters for USFORCECOM staff cadres.

During the first weeks of the grinding Balkans campaign, the old Italian port city had taken on the frenetic and somewhat corrupt air of a rear-echelon location like Saigon during the Vietnam War or London and Paris in World War II. Like those other cities before it, Otranto had become a tenderloin where anything went.

Almost twelve hours after the Osprey made its landing, Saxon was seated at the bar of a local restaurant on Otranto's main commercial strip. The city's shopkeepers, restaurateurs, hoteliers and prostitutes were enjoying boom times of late. The main drags never closed these days, with combat troops eager to forget the fighting in good times, hell-raising, drinking and drugging behind friendly lines.

Saxon made an index-finger-down gesture to his empty bourbon glass, signaling the waiter at the bar to bring him another round. Cobra Force's leader sat by himself and drank alone. He was not much of a drinker, not these days anyway. Alcohol was a false friend, he'd discovered. But, like a whore who knew her business, a brief interlude with old John Barleycorn could sometimes work wonders and cure all ills.

Saxon had shaved, washed his long hair and changed into civilian clothes for the evening. In combat he kept his hair tied in place with a well-worn, sweat-stained bandana, but now he let it hang free. One of the perks of being in special forces was that you didn't have to get a baldie if you didn't want to. Even in the USMC.

He wore black six-pocket pants, a gray turtleneck

and a black leather peacoat he'd bought in Milan during a furlough a few weeks earlier.

Saxon thought about Milan, Florence, Rome and the northern Italian hill towns that lay between them. He had spent his last leave riding the Italian railway all over the place, picking destinations at random off a creased and tattered hotel map as he rolled along. His procedure would be to get off at a town or a city, take a cab to a hotel and see the sights. After breakfast the following morning he'd be gone from there, and it was on to another place. It was a wild two weeks of good food, good wine and no plans whatsoever. Saxon stayed by himself and liked it that way.

Once he was tempted by the streetwalkers of Florence. The women who, since the days of the Renaissance popes, solicited men in the vicinity of the Arno side of the Uffizi museum, were probably the best-turned-out prostitutes in the world. Giving in to temptation, Saxon let one of them pick him up and brought her to his hotel room.

She was eager to please her customer and Saxon was glad that the new anti-AIDS vaccine had been approved for the U.S. armed forces earlier that year.

He awoke before dawn and began packing. The whore asked where he was going. He told her he was checking out and heading for the train station, and that she had better get dressed and leave herself. He gave her a few hundred lire for her trouble and sent her on her way, to go forth and sin again.

Saxon had never asked the girl's name. That kind of thing wasn't important, and she would have lied anyway. Only the things she had done to please him in the night, and the things she had said to him during the act of pleasing, were of any consequence. The rest was the stuff of emotions and Saxon either had none or had them buried so deep they didn't affect him.

He was aware of this difference between himself and others, and so were the rear-echelon staff types who cut the orders to send him out to blow things up and kill people. It was one of his prime job qualifications. Nobody had bothered analyzing it any further. But Saxon's masters used it to their advantage when necessary, without hesitation.

The bartender brought Saxon his drink and he proceeded to sip some cheer from it. The stuff was not half bad. American rye whiskey, not the usual watered-down swill they called bourbon here and served to the tourist trade. At least this stuff had some fire in it. Not much, but some.

Saxon's thoughts now turned to his own personal debriefing—one separate and distinct from the unit debriefing in which the entire team was present. "Personal Inquisition" would have been a better term.

As Saxon had suspected, the heat was turned on almost from the first. You would have thought he was a criminal being grilled by the police at some points. Cobra Force had succeeded where no other U.S. capability, including fighter strikes and TLAMS, had: It had taken out two Macedonian-Serb surface-to-air missile batteries, which had punched a sizable hole in the enemy's ability to shoot down friendly aircraft.

Had it not been for the onset of inclement weather, the team could have gone on to take out another transporter-erector-launcher system. Yet the debriefers were hostile. They wanted to see some blood, and they did—but not his. Having gotten a bellyful of being harassed, Saxon had stood up, punched the CIA spook who was leaning over and shouting in his face and stormed from the room.

Disciplinary action had been threatened, a court-martial promised, the JAG contacted, but Saxon knew that nothing would happen, that it was just bluster by impotent little men with penis envy.

He had made sure that Patient K. had learned about the whole sorry episode. Kullimore had fixed it, assuring Saxon that the enemies of Cobra Force would not have free reign during debriefings any longer. They were off Saxon's back for good, and if any JAG types showed up on his doorstep, he was to feel free to make them eat their little briefcases.

Now, in the darkened bar, Saxon nursed his drink, idly glancing at the TV up on the wall above the bar, which was tuned to an American channel via satellite. Saxon had been away from home for months already and he didn't miss any of it.

The way things were going, America might be the next battlefield for all he knew. The craziness in the streets and in Washington, the mutual hatreds, the greed, the phoniness—it would all have to come a cropper before too long.

Saxon had no illusions about the good old U.S.A. He wasn't in the Marines to save America. The country could flush itself down the toilet as far as he was concerned sometimes.

He was in the military because it gave him the chance to see action, to put himself to the greatest test of skill and strength there was: the test of combat. That was all, and that was all it ever had been for true warriors throughout time. All the rest was window dressing and public relations, no matter what the politicians claimed.

Saxon was idly aware that a woman had taken a seat on the empty bar stool to his right. The perfume telegraphed the gender, and a sideward glance through slitted eyes confirmed it.

Saxon turned back to his dwindling drink. He decided to finish the booze and go. Pretty ladies sitting alone at bars attracted loudmouths, and Saxon had a dull edge of anger throbbing just beneath the surface. He might do something somebody would regret— probably the other guy more than him if it came down to a fight.

He was surprised when the woman turned to him and said, "So, it looks like we meet again."

It took a moment for it to register, but then Saxon recognized her. Colleen Brennan, the fighter pilot the team had rescued in Macedonia. When he'd last seen her, she was as dirty as the rest of the team and didn't smell half as sweet as she did tonight.

She was also all G'd up in civilian clothes—in her case a black cocktail dress—and with makeup on and her blond hair combed straight, she was a knockout.

"Lieutenant Brennan," Saxon said. "You're looking much better tonight than when I last saw you, climbing into a helo on a hot LZ."

"I could say the same about you," she answered him.

Saxon bought them both a round and changed his mind about leaving. He realized he needed some companionship after all. Brennan was a witty conversationalist and, to the extent possible in a public place, they could talk shop and swap stories.

Much later, Saxon saw her to her *pensione*. Like many soldiers, the smart ones anyway, she had managed to make personal arrangements that kept her away from the Marines barracks while on leave. She looked like she was going to say something, maybe invite Saxon inside. But he didn't want to spoil it; he wouldn't have accepted.

What he wanted from women he got from whores and Brennan wasn't that kind of girl. It was better to keep it that way.

"It's been nice," he told her, and extended his hand. She shook it and smiled.

"Same here," she said.

Saxon said good night and walked out, turning his coat collar up against the sudden rain. On some winding street he found a woman leaning against a lamppost. She had on a micro-miniskirt and high-heeled pumps, showing off her legs. The short jacket was unzipped to display the rest of the goods to potential customers.

The woman looked at Saxon. Saxon nodded at her. Not a word was spoken, but she would be at his complete disposal until he awoke, late tomorrow morning, in a dingy room of a seedy waterfront hotel.

# chapter *ten*

Camp Lejeune, North Carolina, was home to the U.S. 1st Marine Expeditionary Force. An isolated section of the sprawling base had been devoted to Cobra Force for billeting, training exercises and testing out new weaponry and operational procedures.

Because of the bad weather in the Balkans, and the heat that had been turned on Cobra by the chiefs of rival units in the Navy and CIA, General Kullimore had decided to return the force to Lejeune for awhile. When things lightened up some, Cobra Force would be sent back into the southern Balkan theater to kick some more ass.

Saxon didn't like cooling his heels back in the States when there was action to be seen overseas. Although he understood that no matter what the big picture might look like, the weather alone would have kept his team out of action for awhile, he also knew that elsewhere the tactical situation had changed.

Saxon sat at his office desk at Lejeune, thumbing bullets out of a 9mm clip and watching them hit the desktop and roll around while he thought things over.

The war in the southern Balkans had heated up in the week since his departure. There had been some new developments. Some good, some not good. The Soviet army had made a major breakthrough in eastern Yugoslavia and now the nonaligned Romanians sitting to their west and to the north of Bulgaria were getting edgy.

In Washington and NATO headquarters in Brussels, there was mistrust that the containment would hold and that the war might spill over into western Europe, turning a regional war into a global one—at least officially. Geographically, only Hungary stood as a buffer between the Balkan conflict and the southern borders of Italy and Austria.

So far the fighting had stayed conventional. But any escalation, any use of unconventional weapons— any type and by any player—might cause NATO states to act unilaterally, forsaking the North Atlantic Treaty and pursuing their own perceived self-interests. If that happened, all bets were off.

Saxon's meditations were shaken up by the sudden ringing of the phone on his desk. When he picked up, his XO, Riggs, announced that the old armor they'd been trying to scrounge up for a live-fire test was at that moment rolling onto the base firing range.

Saxon told Riggs he'd be there right away. He quickly pushed the parabellum rounds lying around

on the scarred top of his metal desk into the mag and
snapped the cartridge into the butt of his non-
regulation Glock 19 semiauto, then snapped the slide
to chamber a standard FMJ bullet, and shoved the
compact plastic-frame weapon into his quick-draw
shoulder holster.

Then he left the office and climbed into a waiting
pickup truck parked outside, one of various vehicles
used by the team to haul gear around and to shuttle
Cobra personnel to various parts of the sprawling Marine encampment.

The firing range was divided into three major
zones. The first was devoted to close urban combat training, hostage rescue operations and counterterrorist engagements. On this section of the range a
number of mock-ups of built-up areas had been
erected, including building facades and a shooting
house that was the equal of a similar facility used by
Delta Force at Fort Bragg.

Also to be found here was the fuselage of a commercial Boeing 747 jumbo jetliner. The permanently
grounded passenger jet was used to practice hostage
rescue and counterterrorist scenarios. It was a little
pockmarked by bullets by this stage, but that just
added to its charm.

Since the Army's Delta Force and the Navy's
SEALs trained for operations such as these, the Marines' own special operations echelon figured they
should develop some dirty tricks of their own to be
used against hijackers when the time came.

The firing range also included both an outdoor pistol and a rifle range, shooting galleries equipped with a variety of different target types. Saxon expected his personnel to put in 500 hours of live-fire exercises with a variety of weapons per month while not on missions, including but not limited to U.S. military-issue firearms. Cobra Force trained on any and every major weapon type they might conceivably encounter in the field.

The arsenal was stocked with virtually every type of small arms and man-portable antiarmor weapon in service throughout the world. The collection was more than just a fancy gun museum. Part of Saxon's training program called for the team to familiarize itself with the workings of each one of the main weapon types and as many of the regionally produced variants as possible.

The team had to be ready to improvise in the field and fight using the enemy's weapons if, for whatever reason, their own were unavailable. Above and beyond that qualification, studies of the different types of small arms fielded by various forces had proven to Cobra Force that there was no point in toting around U.S. military standard-issue when the Soviets or the Chinese or the Israelis made a better weapon for any given job.

Cobra Force usually went into action armed with a mix of weapons. For some types of missions the team favored the bullpup-barreled Kalashnikov AKS-74, for other missions the Colt Commando, for still others the Steyr AUG with its interchangeable barrel configurations, for still others the SITES Spectre or Jati SMGs.

Saxon's philosophy was to match the right weapon to the tactical situation called for by the mission. You didn't use a baseball bat in a hockey game or a tennis racket on a basketball court.

This was the purpose of today's live-fire exercise on another section of the sprawling firing range— getting checked out on the right weapons for the right job. Saxon drove through the close urban combat range and hung a right around some badly pock-marked and flame-scorched brick walls that the team had recently practiced rappelling on.

As he turned the corner, he saw in the distance a cluster of troops and some heavy armored vehicles— a tank and an APC, to be exact—though Saxon hadn't been told exactly what kind of armor had been brought over that morning. He'd find out in a few minutes, though, he knew.

"Yo, boss," Da Noiz sang out. "Mooner and Hirsh really got lucky this time. They somehow convinced 'em to send over a T-72 tank and an old M113 APC. I figured we'd get an old M-60 MBT at best, from the mothball fleet, but not a freakin' Russian main tank."

Saxon watched his men scramble over the heavily armored rolling stock that Mooner and Hirsh had driven several miles to bring to the firing range— where, hopefully, they would soon be reduced to heaps of smoldering scrap metal and burning slag. The vast weapons depot at nearby Camp Pendleton housed a mammoth assortment of heavy-duty war matériel dating back to World War I in some cases. The armor had come from there.

Uncle Sam kept around a lot of obsolete and outdated combat gear to use in training scenarios. The weapons depot was a supermarket for the stuff. They had everything from captured German 88mm howitzers to functional T-62 and T-72 tanks originally owned and operated by Iraq and brought over from the Gulf.

The tank now sitting on the range came from the depot. The M113 was somewhat less of a rare bird. The squat, boxy, tracked armored personnel carrier was of a type that predated the Bradley. The M113 series had been one of the most common APC designs the world over for decades. But Saxon judged that both types of armor would do very nicely as targets for some new ordnance he was about to try out.

S axon took cover behind a triple-rowed heap of sandbags. The live-fire test of the new weapon system that Saxon planned to use on the next SAM-busting mission was about to commence. One of the results of Saxon's after-action reflections on the team's performance in Macedonia had been the idea to use a top-attack weapon against mobile SAM launchers and fixed launchers as well.

The weapon Saxon was thinking of was a new, man-portable version of SADARM (sense-and-destroy armor) under development by DARPA. SADARM was a top-attack weapon system using a brilliant round designed to be fired from artillery or MLRS launchers. The new manpads version, SA-DARM IMP (improved man-portable) resembled other shoulder-fire weapons designed for antiaircraft roles, but unlike these the missile the SADARM fired was specifically designed to track and kill land-based armored vehicles.

When unfriendly armor was sighted in the vicinity, a soldier with a SADARM launcher fired the missile on a vertical or near-vertical trajectory. Once the missile reached its azimuth and tracking altitude, a small ram-air parachute opened and the warhead pointed downward. Thermal and optical sensors and millimeter-wave radars in the warhead hunted for the signatures of tanks, APCs and other armor. This was search and tracking mode, during which the firing crew could control it, guiding it to its target if necessary.

When the signatures were recognized by SADARM's onboard computer, the missile phased into terminal guidance mode. A solid-fuel rocket engine flamed to life and propelled the missile downward toward the top of the target vehicle at extremely high speed. Its shaped-charge warhead exploded within inches of the surface of the armor, punching blast wave and shrapnel into the target with devastating force. A SADARM strike on armor usually resulted in the complete destruction of the armor and crew in a cauldron of fire.

The way Saxon saw it, if SADARM worked against mechanized armor, then it would work even better against the far more vulnerable mobile launchers, which were basically APCs mounted with radars and pneumatically operated launch rails for the missiles they carried.

Cobra Force had been given three reusable

shoulder-fire launchers for SADARM IMP and a supply of missiles, enough for the team to practice on
until it developed proficiency with the weapon.

Saxon reserved the chance to fire off the first SA-
DARM IMP top-attack round himself, though. From
his position behind the sandbag barricade, he hefted
the launcher onto his shoulder, aimed high and fired
the round.

With SADARM IMP, the target wasn't acquired
before, but after, firing the missile. That made firing
it considerably different from other man-portable
rocket launchers like Stinger or TOW, where you had
to put the target between the crosshairs before you
pulled the trigger.

SADARM IMP was an NLOS, or non-line-of-sight
weapon. No need to see the whites of their eyes first.
Just point and shoot.

Still propping the empty and much lighter firing
tube on his shoulder, Saxon stared into the binocular
target scope jutting from the side of the tube. The
missile's parachute had deployed and the round was
slowly drifting to the ground from its ceiling of one
thousand feet in search and tracking mode.

The target scope viewfinder showed Saxon downward real-time imagery of the two pieces of outdated
armor parked on the firing range about five hundred
yards from his position behind the sandbag barricade.
The targeting processors situated just behind the warhead optics of the SADARM round had picked out
the tank and APC from various other junkers and de-
coys that Saxon's Marines had placed around the
range.

But the APC and the main battle tank had been situated too far apart for SADARM IMP to get them both in one single shot. The targeting system had drawn blinking white boxes around the T-72 and the APC framed in the scope, but not around any of the other decoy targets.

*Designate target one or two,* the system scrolled across the top of the viewfield in white characters.

Saxon decided to kayo the T-72 and used the small lever handily located within thumb's reach of the trigger to move a block cursor over the box enclosing the Soviet tank. He clicked on the box and the words *Target number one selected. Confirm* appeared on the screen. Saxon confirmed with another click and the grayscale thermal image of the tank below began to grow larger in the viewfield.

Saxon's pulse quickened. He could also hear the shriek of the missile's engine igniting, propelling the warhead down toward the top of the T-72 with tremendous velocity.

The SADARM round had gone into terminal guidance mode. A split-second later the image of the tank filled the scope's viewfield. The screen went blank, simultaneous with a tremendous boom from the firing range as the munition smashed into the top of the tank and its shaped charge warhead exploded.

Saxon flung the empty launcher to the ground and clambered up to survey the aftermath of the strike over the edge of the sandbag revetment. The devastation was thorough and impressive in its ferocious effects.

The entire top of the tank was completely de-

stroyed, the turret had been knocked off its ring like
a decapitated head, a fireball was rising and bobbing
up into the sky, trailing a dense black cloud of thick,
coiling smoke. As the flames gushed up and died
down, Saxon saw that the body of the T-72 was now
but an empty metal hulk, a chalice of fire and death
offered up to the gods of war.

"Hirsh, get a detail with some foam out there and
douse those flames," Saxon ordered. Portable chemical foam dispensers were available on the range for
rapidly quenching fires caused during weapons testing.

Cobra's commander was greatly pleased by the
performance of the new weaponry. If SADARM IMP
could do this to a tank with no munitions onboard to
cook off in the blast, the fireworks that would be
produced by a strike on a mobile SAM launcher
would be far, far more impressive; like the Fourth of
July compared to New Year's Eve. And the best part
of an NLOS weapon like SADARM IMP was that
the shooter could be up to a mile away from the target
when it went up in a fireball.

The only remaining problem he could see was in
running out of old armored vehicles to shoot at while
training his people in the use of the weapon. Before
the day was out they would need to get themselves
another ration of targets.

Colonel Ness was Patient K.'s chief of staff; while
Kullimore was in the Balkans commanding
troops in the field, Ness performed vital staff func-

tions back at Lejeune. Now, almost three weeks since Cobra Force's return to the States, both the weather and the tactical pictures had begun showing signs of change that would have a direct effect on the future of Saxon and his men.

Ness heard the knock at his office door and told Saxon to come in. Cobra's commander was expected, since Ness had just sent for him.

"Stand at ease, major," he told Saxon. "In fact, sit down."

When Saxon was seated, Ness went on.

"I take it those hellacious explosions I've been hearing all morning are the result of those new NLOS weapons you got from DARPA."

"Yes, sir," Saxon answered. "They certainly are."

"How do they look to you?"

"Sir, they're pure dynamite," Saxon returned. "I think we've got something that can be a really big asset in taking out SAM launchers. Only one thing," he added, trying to appear nonchalant. "We'll probably need some more old armor to practice on. The tank and the APC you got us from Command are pieces of scrap by now."

"Don't worry, Saxon," Ness replied. "I figured you'd be back for more if SADARM IMP worked out. I've already got the orders cut. Just tell me how many and what kind you'll need. It'll be here by tomorrow morning."

"Thanks, sir," Saxon said. Then he told the colonel he'd need another dozen pieces of target armor.

Ness didn't blink an eye. As bad as it got for Cobra outside the ranks, inside the Marine Expeditionary

Unit headquarters, staff support for the force was 100 percent.

The force was Patient K.'s prize special warfare capability, and a historic first for the Marine corps. Within reason, Saxon and his personnel got whatever they asked for, without having to contend with the usual bureaucratic hassles and red tape.

"Now that we've got that out of the way, major, I'll tell you what I asked you to come see me about," Ness went on. "I've got new orders from HQ. You and your men are to saddle up and get ready to go back into the SAM belt.

"A helo will fly you out to the airfield at 0400 hours five days from now. From there a C-130 making a supply run to USFORCECOM will shuttle you to Otranto. You'll get the rest of your instructions there and have a chance to refamiliarize yourself with the big picture before you ship out again. Got it?"

"Yes, sir."

"Any questions?"

"No, sir."

"Then that's it, major. Good luck."

Saxon saluted the colonel and left the office. The team's imminent departure for the Balkans was welcome news, but there was a lot of ball-breaking work still to do before they left. His guys would hate his guts by the time the helo came in for the pickup. He was certain.

But, fuck it, that was what he got paid for.

book two **Black Thunder**

# chapter *eleven*

The craggy northwestern coastline of Turkey is made up of numerous fingers of rocky land that rake the blue Aegean like a gryphon's claw. Between the talons of this claw lie gaps of calm turquoise water forming sheltered coves dotted with many small islands.

By night a freighter, a battered scow under Qatari registry, slid without running lights into one of those numerous coves. On the deck the captain faced the ship's prow. He adjusted the straps of a Russian army surplus night vision rig to the sides of his clean-shaven and waxed head and then fingered the illumination intensity control on its side. The coastline abeam of the ship showed up as a black broken mass against the muted, lighter tones of sea, stone and sky.

Suddenly a flash of light strobed from the Turkish headlands in the distance across the narrowing gap of ocean. The flashing pulse was repeated. It was the signal the captain of the scow had been expecting.

He raised the matte-black tube of an infrared signal gun, aimed it into the night and flashed the reverse of the strobe sequence he had just received. The skipper then removed the night vision rig from his head. He no longer needed it to see the otherwise invisible IR strobes. He knew this coastline like the back of his hand, as he knew many others in the Aegean and the Med.

A short time later, the battered old whore of the seas was moored in the shallow waters off one of the dozen small islets off the coast of Ayalik, Turkey. Several miles away, across the now inky waters of the Aegean, lay the Greek island of Lesbos; the skipper idly watched the faint glimmer of the lights of the hotels and casinos along its *boursi*, or waterfront. All the while the cargo from the freighter's hold was off-loaded and a new cargo laid in from a smaller vessel that had left the protection of the rocky coast and nudged alongside.

The captain turned to his first mate, who supervised two crewman at the winch working the motorized hawser line. One of the crates from the Turkish cruiser swung over the bulwarks and was lowered carefully to the freighter's deck. At a nod from the captain, the first mate went to work with a crowbar on the nailed planks that secured the cover of the crudely fashioned wooden shipping crate.

The pungent, resinous odor of the Turkish opium poppy that had been a faint tang on the sea's salt breeze now overwhelmed the other smells of the sea and the night. The captain picked up some of the contraband and inspected it closely, feeling, smelling and tasting it. It would pass. He nodded his approval to his first mate. The lid of the wooden crate was nailed shut again.

Once the additional load of assault rifles, RPG launchers, mortars, grenades and ammunition that the freighter had carried in from the coast of Thessaloníki received and passed a similar inspection by the swarthy, bearded man commanding the cruiser, the two vessels parted company.

Soon the sequestered cove was silent again, and the faint, distant lights of Lesbos' swank *boursi* were the only sign of human presence amid the shroud of primeval night.


Day came. Some three hundred miles to the northeast, on Macedonia's southern tier, Colonel Vuc Dragunovic climbed aboard the Hip helicraft in the chill air of early morning. The helo lifted off and ascended into the cold crystal-blue sky. Dragunovic smoked one of his American cowboy cigarettes as he watched the landscape flash past below, the smoke soothing him, prompting him to think in a ruminative way.

The mountains appeared serene on the surface, but that serenity was a deliberate and calculated deception. Hidden amid the craggy folds of the mountains;

camouflaged beneath the triple and quadruple canopy of hardy trees; lurking in deep, serpentine caves; and sequestered in a multitude of other hiding places were mobile surface-to-air missile batteries that lay in wait for combat aircraft passing overhead.

Beyond the mountains, not very far to the east and north, the battles between NATO and the Bulgarian-Soviet alliance were being fought to decide the fate of the Balkans. Enemy air strikes were taking place around the clock, as were cruise missile attacks from extreme standoff range.

Here and there, tanks, armor and infantry forces clashed in brief but intense battles for control of strategic positions. Hills, valleys, river crossings, highways: All were the casino chips passed across the green felt table in a high-stakes game for control of the southern Balkans. Whoever ended the game with the greatest number of chips on his side of the table won—and the winner took all.

Dragunovic smoked, gazed downward and contemplated events and problems that lay ahead. He was en route to an inspection of his mobile missileers in the field. From time to time he conducted personal inspections of his field units, but he had stepped these up after the bad weather of the previous month had finally cleared.

NATO overflights of the SAM belt would now be stepped up, he knew. The colonel wanted his forces to be at peak readiness during the course of the coming weeks. This desire had as much to do with the performance of his military duties as the pursuit of his own self-interests . . . interests that had nothing to do with the war.

The colonel had no illusions about the war's outcome. The NATO forces would almost certainly prevail and the final chapter to the crisis in the Balkans, which had begun immediately after the breakup of the Soviet Union, would be written. When that happened, and Dragunovic considered it inevitable, he would need to disappear from his mountain stronghold. Disappear permanently into a comfortable—indeed, lavish—retirement.

Dragunovic estimated that the current war's life expectancy was already growing short. Within a month or two a cease-fire would be declared. Neither the resurgent Soviets nor the Western powers dared risk an escalation of the conflict, and it was obvious to the colonel that the Soviet incursion into Bulgaria merely represented a form of adventurist muscle-flexing of the Kremlin's new military might.

The commissars in the new Russia wanted to advertise their virility to NATO and the United States. They had found a willing pawn in Sofia, where the Bulgarian dream of merging with Macedonia had opened the doors to a massive Russian presence.

In the meantime, while all the fighting in the Balkans was going on, the Soviets had achieved their main strategic purpose in the war—a massive and brutal suppression of secessionist states in the southern Caucasus and on the Iranian and Afghan flanks, and control of Caspian Sea and Black Sea oil reserves.

That was the true purpose for the conflict, as far

as the Kremlin went. All the rest was a bloody little sideshow designed to tie up NATO while the Russian bear cleaned up its den in the southern territories, unhindered by political or military opposition from the West.

Dragunovic was sure that after a bilateral cease-fire was declared, the Bulgarians would retreat from Macedonia. NATO control would fall over the entirety of the Balkans. Global politics and international business would resume its usual pace and money, not battle, would obsess Moscow, Washington, London and Brussels. The world would forget this war and move onto other things, other business and other wars.

For a time at least, everyone would be friends again—except for the necessary scapegoats. The International War Crimes Tribunal in The Hague would need its supply of fresh sacrifices to mollify world opinion and the clamor for vengeance and compensation by self-styled victims of war's brutal excesses.

Dragunovic had no doubt that this time he would find no safe refuge anywhere in the Balkans. Atrocities committed on his orders in Bosnia and Kosovo, sins perpetrated in the name of ethnic cleansing, were on computerized lists in Washington, The Hague and London. Eyewitness had lived to finger Dragunovic. He would be a wanted man, a Cain in search of shelter but denied sanctuary.

No. There would be no escape in the Balkans for the colonel once hostilities ceased. He would need to disappear and retire.

He had made a few million in gold and U.S. currency in arms for drugs and diamonds deals with Middle Eastern clients. But a few million didn't go as far as it used to, even a few million U.S. greenbacks. He would need more, much more, to see his plans through. In fact, he would need as much as he could possibly lay hands on.

The performance of his SAM crews might play a role in that, which was one of the reasons he was making the journey this morning.

The colonel flicked his cigarette into the jetstream generated by the powerful turbine engines on either side of the helo. The mottled green blanket covering the undulating mountains was growing large, resolving itself into a canopy of trees. He spotted the clearing in the near distance, and knew the helo would set down soon.

When the helo descended and put its wheels down on the LZ, the colonel lit another cigarette, exited through the port side door and was saluted by the commander of the missile battery. Dragunovic returned the salute and strode toward the TEL and its crew at attention with his lackey trailing behind.

The F-16/F Fighting Falcons tore across the sky on inbound vectors toward strategic targets on the Macedonian border. The Falcons had rotated and gone wheels-up over a USAF air base at Santa Cataldo, a few miles up the coast from the Marines compound at Otranto, Italy, and drunk their fill from a pair of dedicated KC-10 tanker aircraft—a military version of the McDonnell Douglas DC-10 commercial jetliner with massive fuel bladders substituting for a passenger compartment—orbiting over the Ionian Sea midway between their base and the Albanian coast.

Visibility was good and the skies were clear. Under the day's air tasking order, the time on target (TOT) list for the F-16 mission called for the destruction of an oil refinery plant located near the Macedonian commercial airport of Struga, some 600 miles distant. The target was at the extreme limit of the fighter-bombers' maximum combat range; to further complicate the matter, the daylight mission would have to fly a high-altitude attack profile in order to minimize the risks from unfriendly SAMs.

To carry out their mission the F-16s were loaded to their maximum carrying capacity with heavy ordnance and extra fuel packs. By the time the planes reached their target about half their fuel load would have burned off, and the bulbous fastpacks that held the spare avgas could be jettisoned into the mountains below like the empty shells of huge metal eggs laid by some prehistoric bird of fire.

With hundreds of cubic gallons less fuel and minus the added drag of the fastpacks, the planes would be easier to fly, and there would be less back-sass from the balky control sticks. Once the bombload was away the aircraft would be lighter and nimbler still, and performance would be back up to spec. But now, still on the first leg of their inbound tracks, the planes in the F-16 sortie handled about as nimbly as pregnant brontosauruses as they turned their noses to the sky and fought for altitude.

\*     \*     \*

Colonel Vuc Dragunovic walked around the SAM battery, noting the steps its crew had taken to camouflage the hulking tracked vehicle with tree branches, military netting and earthen berms. The mobile missile tracking and launch system was an SA-10 type, the best of its kind under his command. It was imperative that its crew know how to use it to maximum effect and how to protect it from harm.

The colonel was not as sure of the crew commander, Captain Jan Stulaj. The captain struck him as being accomplished in the art of sniveling and bootlicking but sorely lacking in qualities befitting his military specialty.

Stulaj had been diligent in making certain that his colonel had a lighter flame at the tip of his cigarette each time he started a fresh one, but showed a disturbing lack of leadership and technical knowledge of the SAM system. On the other hand, the young lieutenant who was Stulaj's XO was a sharp one, and seemed to know the system inside out.

It was the lieutenant who had been in charge of the camouflage preparations for concealing the launcher amid the trees. He was proud of these efforts and pleased that the colonel thought the job well done. The lieutenant also had played a large part in making certain that all the electronic and computer systems onboard were in perfect working order, and was eager to show the colonel the crew space inside the APC.

"Sir, if you will step inside, our battle crew will

be pleased to stage a drill we have prepared for you as a simulation exercise."

"Very well," Dragunovic replied. This version of the SA-10 system incorporated simulation and training software in the onboard computer system so that crew could continually drill.

Once inside the tomblike space of the APC's battle cab, the colonel occupied a vacant seat as the lieutenant ordered the two launch officers to activate the exercise routine. The lieutenant stood outside the open door, looking on and narrating events.

"First we have engaged the system to simulate a high-altitude overflight by an enemy fighter strike package," the lieutenant began. "As you can see, sir, we have programmed the system to simulate a three-plane sortie which will enter our zone of radar coverage at a twenty-eight-thousand-foot cruising altitude. This is an average altitude for such a mission, for it will want to avoid SAM coverage."

Dragunovic knew all this but wanted to let the lieutenant take his time explaining. He was watching the young officer with interest and contemplating replacing Stulaj with him if he proved sufficiently worthy.

"Unlike older systems, a high-altitude overflight is no guarantee against a strike from one of the SA-10's missiles," the lieutenant went on. "Not only do the missiles carry more fuel and have longer-range guidance capability, but their warheads are also designed to produce a far more dispersed blast radius than earlier versions.

"Our weapons officers will now engage the simulated aircraft, which you can by now see have already approached to well within the center of our lethality envelope."

Dragunovic studied the radar screen on one of the consoles and saw the icons representing two enemy aircraft slowly creep across the digital map of the region, moving toward the curved edge of a blue balloon.

The threat balloon represented the lethal radius of the four SAMs now loaded on the launch rails of the APC. In only a few moments the planes would traverse the leading edge of the threat balloon and pass within the zone where the missiles could reach them.

"At my command, colonel—" The lieutenant was cut short by a sudden excited announcement from the launch crew.

"Sir! Radar is showing real-world targets approaching on vector Papa-Juliet-Foxtrot-one."

"This is really happening?" the lieutenant asked. "Are you sure it's not the system?"

"Perfectly sure, sir," the launch officer responded. "See?" He changed the viewing mode of the radar to screen out anything that might cause a false-positive contact.

Now the lieutenant was convinced.

"Sir," he announced excitedly to the colonel. "We have an excellent opportunity to show you our abilities in actual combat against enemy aircraft. Shall we proceed?"

"Of course," Dragunovic answered gruffly, though he was inwardly excited at the prospect. "They are the enemy, after all, and it is our business to shoot them down, is it not?"

"Yes, sir. Of course, sir."

The lieutenant rapidly issued orders to the crew, who even now were manipulating keyboards, switches and lighted push buttons, their eyes fixed on the screens before them. The heavy steel door of the APC banged shut and the lieutenant pressed himself into the cramped space of the crew cabin, made even more cramped by the presence of the important visitor from headquarters.

The tension mounted as the icons showing actual aircraft slid along the round face of the scope. Instrumentation sounds filled the cabin, the electronic tones indicating the tracking radar was locked onto the targets.

Moments later the entire vehicle lurched and two of the SA-10 missiles blasted skyward from their launch canisters with a deafening roar. Two new icons joined the symbols superimposed over the moving map display on the radar scope: arrows denoting the airborne missiles.

As the arrows rose toward the unfriendly planes, the aircraft symbols broke formation and engaged in evasive patterns. The path of the inbound missiles changed, as their onboard sensors and the guidance radars on the command vehicle placed the missiles on new attack vectors.

The chase was on, but it was fated to be brief. The F-16 strike package that had taken off from Italy on its way to the Macedonian border was burdened with ordnance and extra fuel, and sluggish in response. By contrast, the warheads streaking up to meet the sortie moved at supersonic velocities.

In moments, two missile and two fighter plane icons collided, and the symbols vanished from the screens. The surviving fighters were already racing away from danger, approaching the opposite end of the SAM threat envelope where they would be safe from harm. It would be pointless to try again with another missile shot. The planes were already out of range.

"Sir, we have two good kills," the lieutenant announced, joyfully and pointlessly, as it was obvious to the colonel from the screens and the jubilant cries of the battle crew.

"I can see that, lieutenant," Dragunovic returned caustically, though pleased with the officer's accomplishment. "Send a search detail to hunt for survivors and wreckage. Anything you find, I want to know about personally from you."

Dragunovic reached for his red crushproof pack of American smokes and popped a cigarette into his mouth.

"Yes, sir, of course, sir," the lieutenant crisply replied, already flipping the lever on a propane lighter to send a blast of flame onto the tip of his superior officer's cigarette.

Dragunovic eyed the face of the young officer as he inhaled, making the cigarette flare.

This one was just what he was looking for, he thought. A combination of efficiency and toadying. In short, a soldier who would go far in his career in the Hugo army. Dragunovic would help him take the next step by promoting him to captain and placing him in command of the mobile missile battery.

*"Personally,"* Dragunovic repeated as the soldier put away the lighter. "Remember that."

# chapter *twelve*

**N**ight. The Osprey that had lifted off from the Marine compound at Otranto flew a southerly course. It transited the Ionian Sea, bypassed Albania and then swung around in a depressed arc over the low mountainous country of northern Greece. Part plane, part helicopter, the Osprey was also outfitted with an air-to-air refueling interface that enabled it to tank up over Greece from a KC-10 fuelbird and continue on its way with full fuel stores.

In the moonless darkness, navigating by INS, the Osprey reached the southern border of Macedonia, translated from front-propulsion to rotorcraft mode, dropped several hundred feet in altitude and began a nap-of-the-earth incursion into unfriendly airspace.

At times flying no higher than 30 feet off the ground, the aircraft remained effectively beneath the curtain of Serbian-Bulgarian ground radar coverage. At that altitude, Doppler echoes intersected like Ping-Pong balls caught in a jet of compressed air, producing an effect called ground clutter. Lost in the static the Osprey was nearly invisible to radar.

The V-22 hastened due north until it reached its destination point, announced by a series of tones from the INS module on the flight deck console. Below, seen through night-vision goggles, the meandering course of the Vardar river flowed slowly and dully in the moonless black of night.

The Osprey's rear ramp swung open and Hirsh kicked a Zodiac out into space, followed by a second Zodiac a minute later. Both black rubber boats landed intact on one of the riverbanks. The helo flared and dropped lower still, skimming the earth like a hunting falcon. Cobra Force jumped off and hit the ground running. The team was in country once again.

It had a mission.

Saxon watched the convertiplane lift off as the pilot manipulated the aircraft's fly-by-wire controls. Showing no lights, the transport aircraft was soon swallowed up in the darkness despite the night vision rig strapped to Saxon's head. The rest of the unit was either standing guard or attending to the preparation of the two Zodiacs for riverine deployment.

Saxon returned his attention to the business at hand. The Osprey had inserted Cobra Force via a roundabout route this time, depositing the team and its gear at a drop zone distant from the area of operations.

Headquarters felt this to be necessary because intelligence assessments of enemy force readiness in the SAM belt showed that special attention was being paid to the western approaches into Macedonia. NATO forces had inserted special operations cadre via those corridors, including Saxon's team. The opposition was now wary and had stepped up patrols after the break in the storm system made more covert actions feasible.

The roughly 200 miles of mutual border shared by Albania, which permitted NATO overflights, and Macedonia, which bristled with fixed and mobile SAM batteries as a buffer against coalition air strikes on Soviet-dominated Bulgaria, was the site of stepped-up enemy patrols.

Troop strength had been increased on the borderlands. These ground troops were complemented by heliborne surveillance teams. The Bulgarian-Serb forces, overseen by Soviet combat advisors, were on heightened alert against the attacks on the Scud farms and SAM installations they knew were sure to come.

But coalition intelligence showed that the southern flank of Macedonia, abutting Greece, was undermanned and still vulnerable to covert penetration.

The opposition obviously didn't consider the possibility that special ops teams would use this corridor as a route inside the breakaway Yugo republic. That was just what had happened, though.

In boot camp, jarheads were taught to be agile, mobile and hostile. The Zodiacs, with their specially designed silenced engines, would glide Cobra Force upriver to a point closer to the known locations of active SAM sites. There the strike team could go to work using its new demolition tools from DARPA.

Saxon's team almost didn't get to go this time, though. The Navy SEALs had gotten wind of the plan for riverine insertion and had tried every maneuver in the book to bump the upstart Marine specwar force from doing the job. The chief of the teams, Rear Admiral Amos "Bud" Dearborn, had forced a meeting between Patient K. and Army General Charles Merrick, the CINC of USFORCECOM.

Dearborn had argued that the SEALS were better trained to run the kind of operation planned for Cobra Force, but Kullimore had shot back that the Marines had a far longer tradition of amphibious operations. Then Kullimore uttered a few magic words that had taken the wind right out of Dearborn's sails:

"Let me name two amphibious operations Marines have undertaken. In the first place, there was an island in the South Pacific called Guadalcanal. Nobody challenged the ability of the Marines to stage such an operation there, or to shed their blood once they got there in defense of our country.

"There was another island called Iwo Jima, in the West Pacific. As I'm sure Rear Armiral Dearborn is aware, the Marine Corps staged amphibious landings here too. Shall I continue, gentlemen?"

There was no need for anything more to be said after that display of oratory. Kullimore had recited the catechism and General Merrick had no option, whatever his preferences, of changing operational plans. Dearborn had left the CINC's office a man beaten in a bureaucratic contest, but Kullimore knew he would be back for another try.

Kullimore realized that the fledgling Marines special operations capability would need constant championing, nurturing and drum-beating in the corridor rings of the Pentagon and the halls of Congress until it proved its worth and became a fact on the ground. Kullimore reflected that his friend and colleague Charlie Beckwith had encountered many of the same problems and resistances in establishing the Army's Delta Force.

Beckwith had been forced to fight battle after battle with bureaucrats and brass in order to maintain Delta. His military career had ended with the debacle in the Iran hostage rescue of 1988, and he had been pushed out of operations into retirement. Nevertheless, Delta had survived that storm and was today that "fact on the ground" that Kullimore pledged himself to make Marine Force One—Cobra Force—into one day.

After Kullimore's meeting, Saxon had been forced into a confrontation with the SEALs on a more physical level than the sharp dialogue between the Pentagon chiefs. Saxon's training and personnel selection methods differed sharply from those of other elite forces commanders. Saxon wanted cool, competent professionals who were as efficient as machines in their jobs. He did not want sick fucks, loudmouths, drunks or prima donnas in his outfit. Others entertained the opposite philosophy, however.

One such commander was Lieutenant Commander Joe Bob Kamms, who headed the SEAL team that had been bucking for the Marines assignment. One of Kamms' SEALs had been drinking heavily at a local bar favored by the Otranto military community and had spotted Saxon with a couple of his sergeants in Cobra Force ordering beers—some of them even "lite" beers.

A phone call from the SEAL quickly brought a crew of SEALs to the bar bruising for a knock-down-drag-out. Saxon proposed an alternative. He would fight Kamms one-on-one, anyplace, anytime, in the ring or out of it.

Kamms was located and a convoy of vehicles was soon headed for a remote stretch of moonlit beach. Saxon studied his rival. He bet himself that Kamms would be eating sand well before the MPs arrived to arrest everyone in sight, which he estimated would be in about twenty minutes.

Kamms took up a karate stance, while Saxon crossed his wrists, placing himself within the triangle of Eskrima, a Filipino martial arts discipline he had been studying with one of its masters; specifically the *sambrada* method, which encompasses counter-for-counter techniques and has many similarities to kung fu, jeet-kune-do, aikido and other related "circular" martial arts forms.

While Kamms went through his kata, Saxon performed *bulong*, mentally enveloping his body in an invulnerable globe of sparkling geometric forms and ethereal white light. Total immersion in *bulong* took a second; having attained this state, Saxon had already won the encounter.

With seeming effortlessness, Saxon countered a combination of hand blows and whirling takedowns with lightning-fast blocks, buffeting Kamms' face with closed-fist knuckle smashes. Kamms retreated, stunned, his lips split, his face bloodied. A SEAL on the sidelines tossed a pair of nunchaku onto the sand, calling out for Kamms to grab the hand weapons. Kamms snatched them up, whirled them around, lunged at his opponent.

The chain-linked hardwood fighting sticks did him no good. Saxon was beneath him, behind him, above him, below him. Kamms stood dumbfounded as Saxon held the nunchaku he had seemingly plucked from his hands as effortlessly as lifting a tissue from a Kleenex box.

Saxon swung the sticks around, demonstrating an expertly executed kata. Then he disdainfully flung the hand weapons away. They were totally unnecessary to taking out his adversary. Only a loser would have resorted to them in the first place.

Saxon now moved quickly, ending the uneven fight with a flurry of hand and foot blows that affected Kamms the way a cattle prod stuns an ox ready for slaughter. Yet Saxon had pulled his punches. He could have easily broken Kamms' jaw, cheekbone or ribs. Kamms was soon sucking up sand with a bloodied mouth as the MPs arrived just like the cavalry in old westerns.

\*     \*     \*

Saxon's brief reverie was short-lived. His mind snapped back to the present at a report from a team member that everything was now good to go.

Cobra Force had set up the Zodiacs, confirming readiness by a round of flashed OK hand signs. The team was already piling its load of gear, weapons and ammo into the inflatables and was ready to push off on Saxon's orders.

Like the biblical Lazarus, he had returned from the dead.

Unlike Lazarus, he had been reborn for a mission of vengeance, totally obsessed with the urge to kill.

He had been medevaced to a regional hospital more dead than alive in the aftermath of the double disaster. His condition was grave at first. The fires of hell had consumed his flesh, seared his nerves, practically cooked the blood in his veins. A quarter of his body had received second-degree burns.

The doctors could do little there but administer morphine for the pain and sterile dressings to the charred and blistered patches of skin. But he had been fortunate. Sofia, Bulgaria, was a helicopter flight away, and the main military hospital there boasted a world-class burn unit.

Lapsing in and out of consciousness from the combined effects of morphine and shock, he was placed in a hyperbaric chamber on arrival at the burn unit and pricked with IV tubes in more places than the sweet potatoes he had supported with toothpicks over glasses of water as a boy in order to make them sprout their pungent green leaves.

The high-pressure oxygen would speed the healing of his terrible burns and wounds; the glucose flowing into his blood through the IV stacks would keep his body and brain alive; the powerful liquid antibiotic that other needles attached to rubber hoses fed into his system would fight off the infection that accompanies severe trauma to body tissue.

Within days he was coherent again, off the morphine and on the weaker drug Percodan to ease his pain. Still, he despaired of ever living a normal life again.

He envisioned going through life with his face covered with hideous pustules and running sores and did not believe the youthful doctors who promised him he would not suffer such a terrible fate. They were lying to him, he knew, to make him more receptive to their treatments, perhaps even to lull him into accepting his oncoming death.

In the end, he knew, nothing would help him. Before he left the hospital and faced an unendurable life as a circus freak, he would find a way to end his life with honor.

There were ways. An overdose of pills perhaps, or slicing open his veins in a bath of warm water, the way defamed Romans of old used to do.

But he had underestimated the young doctors of Sofia. They had been right and he had been wrong. Their ability to heal him was nothing short of miraculous. It had required skin grafts and plastic surgery but the doctors had kept their promise in the end.

He stared into the mirror when the bandages were cut away and his old face looked back at him, just as angular and hard as it had always been. His burned limbs and scalded muscles had responded to physical therapy. Healing drugs and more sessions in the hyperbaric chamber completed the job of mending his broken body. Within a few weeks he was ready to be discharged and ordered to spend the next month in convalescence on medical leave.

Spetsnaz commander Yuri Batalin thanked the doctors and promptly tore up the medical discharge they had given him. He had no intention of going anywhere but straight back into combat, on leave or any other way. The scars and blisters that the flames had raised on his body might have been healed by the medical wizardry of the doctors, but they could do nothing about the emotional and mental scars that remained.

Those only Batalin himself could erase—erase using the blood of his enemies as a healing salve. He was haunted by the images and the sounds of his dying comrades in the one-sided firefight with the American commando force.

The stench of their burning bodies still clung to his body, filled his nostrils, stank up his mind. He had not slept soundly since the disaster. He knew he would never sleep soundly again until he had succeeded in exacting revenge on those who had shamed him as a warrior and slaughtered his comrades like wolves amid the sheepfold.

When Batalin checked himself out of the hospital he went directly to the military air base at Pernik and managed to get himself aboard a transport helicopter ferrying supplies, spares and ammunition to Macedonian-Serb forces in the interior of Macedonia. Within a day he presented himself to his commander, Vuc Dragunovic, in the warlord's underground head-quarters.

"I am fit for duty," he reported. "I request permission to resume the hunting and destruction of enemy commandos with which you originally charged me."

Dragunovic didn't hesitate a second.

"Permission granted," he replied, blowing cigarette smoke through his nostrils like some kind of medieval dragon.

Batalin proceeded at once to gather a force of Spetsnaz commandos and undertake his mission. He would taste the enemy's blood. He would drink it down. This he promised himself.

## chapter *thirteen*

**C**obra Force made the upriver journey under cover of darkness. Their eyes looked out at the night through light amplifying binocular scopes, scanning the riverbanks for signs of hostile forces. The silenced Zodiacs functioned well, their high-performance engines barely audible as they propelled the inflatables upriver to the team's final waypoint.

The team's destination and target site was a mobile SAM battery that had been identified from satellite photos and SR-71 Blackbird photointelligence. The battery consisted of two launchers, one a low-to-medium altitude SA-8 Gecko and the other a high-altitude SA-10 Tombstone missile emplacement.

Saxon, like the other members of the team, flashed back on the briefing sessions back at Otranto. The large, flat-panel, high-definition screen in the briefing room was linked in real time to an Improved Crystal photointelligence satellite. As the satellite's orbit brought it over the southern Balkans, the team enjoyed a God's-eye view of the territory below.

The resolution was spectacular, although in normal imaging mode the mobile launchers that had been well-camouflaged and hidden were difficult to make out. But when the feed was switched to thermal imaging mode, they could clearly recognize the bulky oblong shapes of the tracked vehicles and see members of the crew that tended the SAM launchers moving around, even make out the glowing tips of cigarettes being smoked.

Ferret birds—signals intelligence satellites—had also been tasked to monitor radio transmissions between the missile crews and their local and regional command centers as well as between one another. The ferrets were orbital listening posts using extremely long antenna arrays as scoops for transient electromagnetic pulse standard radio and microwave transmissions, known by the acronym TEMPEST to intelligence personnel.

RC-135 and AWACS aircraft had dedicated links to ferret telemetry. The planes flew racetrack courses at safe distances from enemy countermeasures, including SAM strikes. Onboard, teams of defense intelligence analysts pored over the multiple gigabytes of data that flowed in from these electronic eavesdropping sources, using high-speed computers to filter the raw data for key words and phrases that might yield useful intelligence product.

The operational picture that swam into focus as a

result of this intelligence gathering showed that security around the Macedonian-Serb SAM batteries had been considerably stepped up. In the aftermath of the raids staged weeks before by Cobra Force, and the blizzard conditions that followed, mechanized and mobile troops had been assigned to patrol the SAM belt.

Airborne patrols were also in place. These were mostly heliborne forces, a mix of gunships, transport helos and light spotter aircraft that conducted aerial security overflights of the central mountainous region of Macedonia where the clusters of missile TELs were in operation.

Saxon's thoughts ran in reverse along the mental tether to the past, and his mind snapped back to the present with crystalline focus. The night was clear and the black bowl of the sky was flecked with deep blue, bright yellow and intense white stars.

The crew observed operational silence, keeping all communication to a minimum, using hand signals or tapping out wireless E-mail messages on their wrist-top data-entry pads when necessary. The specially muffled diesel-electric engines that propelled the Zodiacs upriver made only the faintest chugging sound. They did not use propellers but instead worked on the hydrojet principle, rapidly forcing a stream of water out a tube under high pressure as a method of propulsion.

Other than the sloshing of water against the sides of the inflatables and the barely audible creaks made by the expansion and contraction of the high-strength latex polylaminate of which the inflatables were constructed, there was only the keening of the wind and the rustling of the trees and the sounds made by nocturnal animals hidden in the forest beyond the riverbanks.

Saxon and his Marines knew, though, that the tranquility of the night was cruelly deceptive, and that it could become their downfall if they permitted themselves to be lulled into false security. In an unguarded moment that tranquility could turn into pure, unmitigated hell.

The mountains shouldering the river harbored not only fox and deer but also enemy troops. Cobra's situation was highly vulnerable; secrecy, its greatest asset.

Once under cover in the woods the team's survival chances would increase, but out in the open they counted on the unexpectedness of their inbound route for safety. All it would take was a single random patrol to spot them and they could quickly become overwhelmed by superior force. The precariousness of the situation was not lost on any member of the team.

Still, Saxon could not help but play back the past as the team moved upriver. He thought fleetingly of Colleen Brennan, and of their chance encounter in the bar in Otranto. Colleen's pretty face morphed into the face of the streetwalker he had picked up and used as a surrogate that night. Then it went through another change to become that of his ex-wife.

Saxon had not seen Tamara or his son Wolf in

years. It was better that way. He'd met her while
stationed in Weisbaden, Germany, in the early nine-
ties. In those days Saxon was still under the illusion
that there was something left in him to give to a normal relationship with a woman, let alone a family.

The demons that drove Saxon were his true family.
They, and they alone, called the shots. He recalled
that on the night he and Tamara had met at a disco
in Berlin there had been an old Steppenwolf tune
blasting over the sound system. The lyrics John Kay's
gravel voice was singing had something to do with a
man whose women burn like moths in a flame. Tamara had looked into his eyes and told Saxon she bet
he was like that. It was an inauspicious remark, because it was true, and because that flame had in time
burned their marriage to a cinder.

In the movies the special forces guy's wife is usually killed by terrorists and he goes after the killers
to exact revenge. Nothing like that happened to
Saxon. His work consumed him and taxed his ener-
gies. There was nothing left to devote to family life.

The marriage was disintegrating. Had bad guys executed his woman in a terrorist strike, Saxon would
have undoubtedly tracked them down and tacked
their heads up on the Berlin U-bahn, but he would
have done so emotionlessly and then moved on. But
it was nothing that romantic. He had just had it with
being married to Tamara. That was it. That was all.

One day Saxon deposited most of his savings in a
bank account for Tamara and whatever valuables he
possessed in a safe-deposit box. He left a note with
the details and the key to the box in their apartment.

Then he left his wife and child. Walked out. Simple as that.

He had never heard from them since and had never tried to contact them. He hoped they were all right, but he was honest enough with himself to admit that he didn't care one way or the other. They were probably better off without him anyway.

Two tones, one high, one low, sounded in Saxon's ear. His pulse quickened and his attention jogged back to the present. These were alert tones, giving advance warning of an impending threat condition.

"Arcade to Kingsnake. Over."

The call-sign was from the mission's dedicated AWACS support. The airborne warning and control system plane was specially outfitted with satcom pods and special fairings to enable it to communicate with an array of orbital surveillance satellites, but also to transmit messages and multimedia data via the Milstar satellite network to Cobra Force in the field.

There was no need to acknowledge the transmission. AWACS knew the team was observing operational silence.

Arcade proceeded, "Threatcon Hammock warning. Mi-24 gunships approaching your position on a north-northeast vector. ETA five minutes. Advise immediate defensive action. Acknowledge only for message repeat."

Three hundred miles away, at the extreme limits of communications range, even using non-line-of-sight satellite relays for over-the-horizon radio transmission, the spook manning one of the consoles in the high-security area of the cabin had an Olympian view of the situation on the ground.

The Improved Crystal satellite imagery was not anywhere near the limits of its zoom resolution, but still it covered a 30-square-mile radius. Within its coverage area the NSA signals intelligence engineer watched as two Mi-24 Hind helicopter gunships, nicknamed Devil's Chariots, approached the bend in the river where the Zodiacs were presently located.

The scope man remained professionally and emotionally detached from the situation in-theater. By temperament and by occupation he remained cool under stress. He scanned the image area and adjusted the field of focus. He then made a quick calculation and keyed his mike.

"ETA now three minutes to contact," Arcade advised the team. "Suggest you make for cover of railway bridge around the next bend in the river. At maximum speed you should be in range in about half a minute."

The Zodiac engines would not perform as quietly under full throttle, but this was an emergency. The Marines goosed the throttles and the inflatables surged forward. Saxon, in the lead Zodiac, was one of the first to spot the railway trestle span in the darkness ahead of them.

The trestle bridge loomed up around the bend, just as Arcade had said. In the shadowy recesses beneath its flexed steel buttresses the team might find a place to hide from the gunships. Otherwise the heavily armed Mi-24s packed enough firepower to snuff them

MARINE FORCE ONE          151

like a nest of insects, or failing that, blow their cover
for every Yugo trooper in the region with a single
radio alert.

Now the team heard the engine and rotor noises of
the onrushing gunships echoing off the darkened
hills. The sound at first was a low, ominous chugging.
But within a matter of seconds its volume increased
to the point where the telltale *thuk-a-thuk-a-thuk* of
dishing helicopter rotorblades was plainly audible.

As the team gained the dubious safety of the bridge
and, under Saxon's orders, spaced themselves out
along the concrete and steel buttresses on either riverbank, the noise of the approaching helo became a
deafening roar, pierced by the high-pitched shriek of
the port and starboard turboshaft engines that sup-
plied cyclical thrust to the helo's main and tail rotors.

Saxon gripped his Commando assault weapon, not
knowing what to expect, and scanned the skies
through the steel lattice of the overhead trestle. A
cold fear gripped him as the gunships paused and
hovered over the bridge area instead of continuing
their overflight of the river and scudding off into the
night.

Could the pilots have seen the team? he wondered.
Or had they been alerted to the presence of the riverine force by someone else, known Cobra Force's
approximate position in advance of arrival? Either alternative was possible, although it was also likely that
the helos had paused for some other reason having
nothing to do with the team's presence.

Saxon could not fathom what that third alternative
might be as he kept his eyes fixed on the two killing

machines that hovered just a few dozen feet above their heads. Like the rest of the crew, all he could do was wait and will himself into invisibility, will the airborne predators away from the strike team's vulnerable position beneath the rail trestle.

Suddenly a new sound began to insinuate itself into the audial surround. It was a distant, oncoming rumble that steadily grew in intensity as the seconds multiplied. With the approach of the sound the trestle bridge began to vibrate and then start to sway, its vibrations passing down into its massive buttresses and making the inflatables rock to and fro in tidal forces imparted to the water.

A train was coming, about to cross the bridge, the Marines knew. But as the diesel locomotive negotiated a low grade onto the trestle bridge, the vibrations increased to the point where the inflatables were in danger of capsizing.

The rubber Zodiacs were heavily laden with personnel and gear, their weight load carefully calculated and precisely balanced. They were not intended to be subjected to the intense vibrations of an express freight barreling overhead and making the earth shudder. Saxon and the rest fought to keep their balance and prevent the Zodiacs from turning over, spilling men and equipment into the river and alerting the unfriendly helos to their presence.

Now the freight train had mounted the bridge and was passing directly above them at high speed—too high, in fact. Saxon guessed the train driver was deliberately pushing the throttle, maybe just to experience the high of speed and danger, or enhance the effect of drugs.

Saxon kept his eyes on the helos. They were still hovering above the bridge, darting like dragonflies, but now, with the approach of the inbound train, they began to swoop back and forth over the express freight which replied to their antics with sharp blasts on its powerful air horn. The shrill wail echoed off the hills and water, deafeningly loud, a chilling presence in the night.

More than the additional noise of the air horn now afflicted the team. The steel wheels of the speeding train had begun throwing off hot, crackling, blue-white friction sparks as they rolled and scraped across the iron rails.

Some of these incandescent metal cinders went tumbling over the side of the trestle, landing on the rubber skin of a Zodiac and immediately attacking the rubber. The crew struggled to brush off the sparks, praying that the attention of the helo crews was not drawn down toward them by the fiery cascade.

The vibrations were now at highest intensity as the line of boxcars rumbled directly overhead, fast and straight across the trestle. The game of aerial cat and mouse with the diesel continued, the Devil's Chariots dipping and swooping like disturbed bats in the black night air.

The Zodiacs were buffeted by sloshing river water, and Saxon's inflatable was nearly pulled from its moorings alongside the buttress. Hirsh's team was having even worse trouble. Saxon saw equipment spilling into the river as the other inflatable listed sideways.

In moments it would be all over, Saxon feared. The helos could not fail to notice the commotion, sweep in, sight their targets and open up with their guns. But the train had almost passed completely now, and the fierce shaking of the bridge had ebbed considerably. There was a final toot on the locomotive's air horn, and then the rumble of the freight began to recede into silence and distance, leaving only the coffee-grinder sound of the helos overhead.

Then Saxon saw that they too were leaving the scene. It had been the oncoming freight that had caused them to hover over the bridge. They had seen the train approaching along the rail line and had decided to have a little fun, play a game of tag. Maybe that was why the freight had been running so fast— it might have been a regular game the driver played with the helo pilots.

One thing he was sure of: The helos had not been looking for the team and had not had intelligence concerning its location. To Saxon's immense relief, the helos soon climbed for altitude and sped off into the night. In seconds they had vanished completely.

Cobra had escaped death by a slim margin, but the team had not emerged unscathed by the encounter. One of the Zodiacs was badly damaged and had to be hastily patched in places where hot sparks had melted holes in the rubber. Worse yet, there had been an unknown quantity of gear lost in the black, cold waters of the river.

The unit would not know what precisely had been

sacrificed until it could establish its mission support site at a secure place on land. But whatever turned out to be missing, the fact was that any loss was bad. Any loss whatsoever. The team had carried a precisely calculated load of gear in country and the absence of even a single bullet might well prove dangerous to the mission—and to their lives.

# chapter *fourteen*

Cobra Force navigated the Vardar river without further mishap. The Marines special operations unit reached its scheduled land debarkation point approximately seven miles from the site of the TEL farm they planned to take out.

The black Zodiacs were dragged clear of the water and onto the grassy verge of the riverbank and the team's gear and weapons removed. The boats were then deflated and buried. The team would have no further use for the inflatables; their extraction would be heliborne.

With each team member loaded down with a 50-plus-pound pack, the Marines began a hump toward the scheduled location of what was to be the mission support site for their countermissile battery operations inside Macedonia. The air was crystal clear but temperatures hovered around the freezing mark, with a wind chill making it feel considerably colder than it really was. It would soon be summer in this hemisphere, but winter had not yet given up its iron grip on the frozen land.

In the hours of darkness left before twilight, the team reached the predesignated hide and mission support site. Though they were tired from the march, there was still considerable work to be done before the arrival of full daylight.

First, the site had to be prepared for occupation. A security force was posted by Saxon to patrol the woodland perimeter while the rest of the team got out entrenching tools and began to dig a tree-pit shelter for bivouacking, mission support and observation.

A suitable tree, branches still covered with an earlier fall of snow, and situated close to the ground, was located, and the team began clearing a thirty-foot circular pit around the circumference of the tree trunk. Snow was then packed down hard around the top and the inside of the pit to provide added support for its earthen walls. The low, sloping branches of the pine, especially those covered with an incrustation of refrozen snow, provided a natural mottled pattern that afforded good cover from observation.

The team enhanced this natural camouflage by cutting evergreen boughs and draping them over the top of the pit for additional overhead masking. Communications antennaes were easily and effectively concealed within this layered umbrella of foliage, debris and snow that surrounded the sides and covered the top of the pit.

By the time the mission support site was satisfactorily completed, the twilight had come and gone and the false dawn that precedes full daylight was inching its way across the land. The MSS would be home to the entire team for the next twelve hours as it rested and staged a remote reconnaissance of the strike zone via satellite and unmanned aerial vehicle imaging.

Moving patrols would be posted in the vicinity to guard the hide site; these would be rotated every two hours to give the entire team a chance to grab some rest, chow and downtime. Still, the hours that remained before action could hardly be considered as offering repose to anyone but troops hardened to the rigors of functioning in a combat environment. The hide site was cramped, cold and claustrophobic, and the team shared its shelter with grubs, beetles, worms and sharp-edged rocks.

Cobra had to observe strict operational silence, speaking only when necessary and even then communicating in whispers. The team's personnel also had to keep their weapons constantly within reach and their helmets always on. The unit had to consider itself under imminent threat of discovery by the enemy and be ready to engage Yugo troops in a firefight at a moment's notice.

Even so, those Marines on rest break immediately fell asleep. It wasn't just that they were bone-tired. It was because they were Marines and they had been here before.

\*    \*    \*

Marko Petrovic, a Yugo private second-class, paused from a long march to slake his thirst at the edge of the river. Cupping his hand and scooping up a few ounces of clear river water, he rinsed the foul taste of tobacco from too many chain-smoked filterless Russian-made cigarettes from his mouth. When the soldier spat into the stream, he noticed an object bobbing in the eddies of a rocky outcropping a few hundred feet from his position.

His attention caught, the Yugo trooper shaded his eyes to better see what it was. It looked like a box or crate, seemed black or dull green against the swift-flowing current. He wondered what it might be, and if it held anything of value. Like all the other troops in Macedonia, the soldier was ill-paid when he got paid—and sometimes wasn't paid at all.

Petrovic's uniform was frayed in places, and patched in others, from months in the field, and many miles of slogging had badly worn his combat boots at the soles. Like all other Macedonian regulars, Petrovic used the black market as a way to compensate himself for the privations of doing military service in the Yugoslav army.

Stepping carefully over the treacherously wet rocks along the bank of this part of the river, Private Petrovic knelt and examined the floating object before attempting to touch it. For all he knew it could be a mine or a booby trap of some sort, perhaps dropped by NATO planes or helos.

Close up, Private Petrovic recognized the object as a milspec ammunition caisson. The reinforced plastic storage box was painted in a woodland scheme that was immediately recognizable as different than the Yugoslavian woodland camouflage pattern. Petrovic also noticed the stenciled writing in black on the ammo box. He couldn't read what it said, but it looked like English to him. Moreover, he recognized the acronym "USMC." That meant the United States Marine Corps.

Private Petrovic wondered what in hell the ammo box was doing floating in the river but decided against the probability of it being a booby trap or a mine. Fishing it out of the water was another problem, though. At first it bobbed tantalizingly close, though remaining just outside his grip, so that in overreaching he almost plunged ass-over-teakettle into the icy-cold river water.

Cursing as he snapped back to a standing position, Petrovic regained his balance and used the barrel of his AKS-74 to try nudging his discovery closer. The watertight box still eluded all his efforts to recover it, floating irritatingly out of reach.

In frustration, Petrovic changed tactics. Laying aside his assault rifle, he found a long section of dry tree branch lying amid the rocks of the riverbank. Using the much longer branch, this time Petrovic was successful in propelling the box over to the edge of the river rocks. Lifting it was another matter, as it was heavy; far heavier than he would have thought, in fact.

Finally he dragged his prize a few feet onto the bank and unsecured the series of latches that fastened down its lid. Peering inside, the private saw that the box was packed with hand grenades.

Petrovic was overjoyed. *Here* was a treasure trove! He could sell the grenades on the black market for a tidy profit. Closing the lid, he hid the box in a thicket of brush near the river and returned to his unit's encampment. He would ask his sergeant, who was his black market contact, what he might be willing to pay for what he had just discovered.

Yuri Batalin dismissed the sergeant and turned his gaze, and his mounting wrath, on the private who now stood alone with him in his office. Private Marko Petrovic's terror at being on the receiving end of the powerfully built NCO's anger, threats and accusatory questioning was double now that his companion had been dismissed.

Petrovic remained at rigid attention. The Spetsnaz noncom had not yet given the private permission to stand at ease in his presence. In any case, Petrovic was far too petrified to comply with such an order, even if given.

Batalin paced back and forth across the room until, stopping in mid-stride, he stood eyeball to eyeball with the private. Batalin stared hard into the young conscript's ashen face. Although the soldier strained to maintain a martial bearing, Batalin could see he was coming apart under the grilling.

"How do I know you are not a spy for the fucking Americans?" he shouted at the private. "Give me one reason for not shooting you right now as a spy and a traitor."

To show the soldier he wasn't playing games with

him, Batalin pulled his service pistol and brandished it in front of the detainee's face. Beads of sweat stood out on the private's forehead as his eyes crossed along the barrel of the gun. Batalin wanted to burst out laughing at the pathetic sight, but was too good an actor to show his true emotions.

"Sir, I am no traitor," Petrovic stammered in reply. "I found this box in the river. I am innocent of any crime."

"No? You say are innocent. You claim you are not a traitor. You declare you are no spy. And yet there is this box of American ordnance which you, through your superior, tried to sell on the black market. Is that not the act of criminals?"

"Sir, all the other men trade—"

"Silence!" Batalin barked, shutting up the private immediately. "Did I ask you for an answer, private?"

"No, sir. Sorry, sir. You did not."

"Then listen. As I began to say, selling contraband on the black market is a crime punishable by court-martial. Whether or not the whole fucking world does it is beside the point. You and your comrade have admitted to it. You will face disciplinary action.

"Fortunately for you, I do not believe you are a spy or I would have shot you already." Batalin holstered his pistol, seeing the relief on the private's flushed, sweaty face. "And that is for the sole reason that you have impressed me as being far too stupid to be a spy. Now get the fuck out of here. You are dismissed. Never let me hear your name again or I will reconsider my decision."

"Yes, sir. Thank you sir," the private blurted, almost tripping over his feet in an effort to leave the presence of this demon from hell who had tortured him for almost an hour.

When he was alone in the marshalling room, Batalin sat on the side of a table and lit a cigarette. Inhaling the first strong drag of Turkish tobacco smoke, he exhaled and studied the flaring tip of the cigarette between his bunched knuckles. His mind drifted as the cone of lengthening ash grew by imperceptible degrees.

The Spetsnaz commander had never entertained even a second's doubt concerning the loyalty of the two soldiers. He had used fear as a bludgeon to beat every last iota of information about where and how the ammunition container had been found from their minds. They had told him everything they knew. Unfortunately, however, it wasn't much.

In his mind's eye, Batalin saw a map of the region where the box had been found. The location was in one of the bends of the Vardar river, which drained down from the high mountain country. It had probably floated downstream from a higher elevation.

Where had this boxful of grenades come from? He doubted it had fallen out of an American transport, as the terrified soldiers would have had him believe. More likely that it had been lost by a U.S. special forces team bound in-country, a successor to the teams that had been operating in the SAM belt before the weather had turned grisly. The presence of the box argued for a riverine insertion this time, the Spetsnaz believed.

Such a strategy would make perfect sense. The

Western coalition's special forces were expected to attack from the obvious corridor, striking westward, from Italy and across Albania, not northwestward, from northern Greece. This latter course would require considerable overland travel by troops bound for the thickest sectors of the SAM belt where the largest missile batteries were to be found. Yet coalition special forces would certainly strike again, because NATO was surely aware that the last commando strikes had paid back operational dividends.

In the sector where at least one American special forces outfit had struck, a critical part of the surface-to-air missile barrier protecting Bulgarian airspace from NATO attacks had been decimated by surgically precise commando strikes. Those same commandos had been responsible for the deaths of most of his Spetsnaz and his own near-destruction in a firestorm of death at the helo crash site.

Batalin dragged deeply on the now half-smoked cigarette and stared into the Dante-esque miniature of glowing ash. Amid the incandescent orange ember the sights, sounds and smells of the attack all came back to him. The death cries of his comrades and friends still haunted him. He heard them in his dreams, he heard them while wide awake. He would not forget them his whole life long.

For a moment the Spetsnaz chief considered the remote possibility that the same band of American Marine commandos that had been responsible for the cowardly attack at the crash site might be the ones who had left behind the artifact that Petrovic had found afloat in the river. In the end he dismissed it as too far-fetched a possibility.

Still, he would recognize those commandos if he ever saw them again, for they operated differently from other Western formations with whose tactics he was familiar. He had not even known prior to the fateful encounter that the Marines even fielded such special operations cadre; he had only heard of this later, while recovering in the hospital.

Batalin took a final drag on the cigarette, dropped it to the floor and crushed it flat beneath the steel toe of his combat boot. There was no more point in reverie. Whatever would happen would happen. He was out of the hospital and back doing the only job that meant anything to him, that of a professional soldier.

All he knew, and all he really cared about, was that there was a strong possibility that U.S. or NATO special forces elements had once again inserted for countermissile battery operations, and it was his job to stop them from carrying out their mission.

The next thing that the Spetsnaz commander needed to do was to attempt to trace the debarkation point of the team from the river, for that would give him a better notion of their general line of march. Once he knew this, he could track the foe with merciless efficiency. Perhaps there were more artifacts, more clues, to be found floating in the river, and perhaps he might even find the place where the inbound team had buried their inflatable boats, for they would have certainly done so once emerging from the river.

The Spetsnaz would issue instructions for search teams to comb the riverbanks. They would be ordered to report directly to him, and to no one else.

Leaving his office, Batalin went to the training area where the new Spetsnaz platoon he had assembled and trained were conducting parade drill. At the commander's approach, the noncom directing the troops ordered them to halt, shoulder arms and stand for inspection.

"Attention!" he shouted.

The troops stood rigidly still, eyes front.

"Present arms!"

The troop cradled their government-issue AKS-74 automatic rifles, heads level, spines straight, bodies erect.

Batalin lit a fresh cigarette and returned the drill instructor's crisp salute, then turned to face the assembled ranks of soldiers. Since getting out of the hospital he had devoted most of every waking day toward selecting, training and outfitting his new Spetsnaz. He had handpicked all of them, poring over service records until he was bleary-eyed, interviewing applicants and weeding out the weaklings, the fools, the cowards and the slackers.

Once he had made his choices, he further winnowed out the deadwood by subjecting them to rigorous combat range testing in which their physical stamina, courage, marksmanship, survival instincts and will to succeed at any price were tested to the fullest.

Those who dropped out were immediately sent back to their regular units without prejudice. The small core of redoubtable men who could take anything thrown at them and come back fighting harder and fiercer and before, those men were the ones that Batalin retained for his new Spetsnaz force.

Now the conscripts were fully proficient and ready to be fielded under actual combat conditions. They were still green around the gills, for they had not yet been seasoned by the rigors of actual combat, and these, Batalin knew, nothing devised by the military mind could come near to duplicating. But at the same time he had no doubt that this green wood would be seasoned by a good, thorough blooding once combat actually began.

The Spetsnaz leader spun on his heels and began moving along the line of troops that stood at attention. One by one, he gazed into their faces, staring hard into their eyes to gauge the level and intensity of their determination and toughness.

Not a man flinched, and each met their commander's flinty stare with one that blazed with equal ferocity. As he completed his review, Batalin was satisfied. In their maroon berets and field-patterned camo BDUs they were the epitome of a superb fighting force, easily a match for any commando unit that any enemy might field to oppose them.

Soon, he surmised, they would have a chance to prove their mettle against the foe in battle. Although he had pushed the men to their limits and beyond, he had never been dishonest with them and he knew he had earned their respect and trust. One of the secrets of being a good commander lay in combining the carrot with the stick, Batalin knew.

Now he reached into his pocket for what he thought of as a cube of sugar.

"Which one of you is the best marksman in the platoon?" he shouted. None answered, and Batalin understood that none wished to put himself before his comrades. This was good, and so Batalin helped things along a bit.

"Vladimir—step out of line," he ordered.

"Sir."

"I have watched you shoot. Do you think you could put a hole through this?"

Batalin held out a gold Krugerrand, taken from among his personal valuables.

"I can try, sir."

"I did not ask that. I asked if you could do it."

"Yes, sir." The barked reply resounded. "I can do it!"

"Good. If you succeed, you and your comrades will enjoy a round of beers on me." A cheer rose from the ranks. Batalin turned back to Vladimir. "Now. Watch. On three."

Batalin counted down and flung the Krugerrand high into the air. It rose to a height of fifteen feet or so and then began to drop again, spinning around and around as it plunged to earth. By the time the whirling gold disk had ascended to the top of its curve, Vladimir had brought the weapon to his shoulder, aimed, tracked on the rapidly falling coin and triggered a single round.

Struck by Vladimir's bullet, the coin jumped in midair like something alive. Another, still louder cheer rose from the ranks at the well-placed shot. Batalin, smiling inwardly but keeping his face firm, dispatched Vladimir to retrieve the coin.

Minutes later the Spetsnaz commander strode up and down the ranks holding up the gold piece so all the men could see where a neat hole had been punched just off-center by Vladimir's expert marksmanship.

Completing his strutting promenade, Batalin handed the pierced Krugerrand to Vladimir and dismissed the entire troop, which headed with enthusiastic shouts in the direction of the base commissary to claim the prize that the marksman had earned for it. Vladimir, at the center of the group, was the hero of the hour.

Batalin watched his young lions in their innocent yet warlike jubilation, wondering how many of those same fledgling warriors would still be alive by the end of the month.

# chapter *fifteen*

**H**irsh, Da Noiz and C.W. crawled like land crabs across cold, moist earth, adding bits and pieces of Mother Nature to the camo patterns on their BDUs; the black, brown and green cammie paint on their faces and similar color schemes on their gillied-up assault weapons and helmets.

The three Marine special operators reached the top of the hillside and flattened down at the crest. Below them an unpaved track branched off a winding stretch of blacktop, leading straight as an arrow into a mountain meadow dotted with groves and small stands of hardy trees.

Here, amid the thickets of pine, elm and spruce, a mobile missile crew was engaged in counter-tacair operations. The SAM battery was an SA-10 type, with the characteristically fat launch canisters for the

48N6 missiles occupying the rear of the half-tracked platform, and the slab antenna of the Flap Lid radar system scanning the dark skies on a 360-degree arc.

The transporter-erector-launcher crew was not the only military force in the meadow below the Cobra Force mobile team. The TEL crew was protected by a security detachment of Yugo mounted infantry of approximately platoon strength. The mounted crunchies had a BMP-3 at their disposal.

An armored fighting vehicle of fairly recent issue, the Bimp bristled with weapons, including a heavy machine gun and hedgehog grenade launchers, and was also thickly armored. A staff car, armed with a .50 caliber machine gun mounted on a pintle stand at the truck's rear, was also available for mobile operations.

The three-man Cobra Force detachment's mission was to wait and assess. A screening and security force, deployed on the recon crew's rear flank, operating in the woods beyond the hill-slope where the three commandos lay hidden, provided insurance against surprise detection and assault by any enemy patrols that might be operating in the area.

These two elements were in communication with the MSS via secure radio links and received regular updates from the command post, which was in turn linked to high-flying UAVs and Improved Crystal satellite feed.

Cobra Force conducted its field reconnaissance using a combination of Land Warrior digital technology and adroit fieldcraft. Roughly half of the covert force remained in position at the mission support site, which combined the roles of remote observation facility and command post.

Under Saxon's direction, the other element of the team functioned as a heavily armed and highly mobile forward observation detachment. Its secondary function was as a strike force whose mobility and firepower gave the three-man squad the commensurate lethality of a platoon of enemy troops.

A cadence of muted alert tones sounded in the ears of the reconnaissance party deployed on the hillside.

"Heads up." It was Jeckyll's voice over SINC-GARS radio. "The UAV's picked up a Yugo heliborne patrol approaching your vicinity."

Hirsh tapped the AFFIRM key on his wrist-top comm rig to respond without breaking operational silence. *What is approach vector and ETA?* he continued to tap out.

"The chopper is approaching you guys from due south. My guess is they'll be on top of you in five."

Hirsh hit the AFFIRM key, then the OUT key. The message was understood and the recon team would take defensive action: hunkering deeper into the protective cover of the margin of trees in which they had positioned themselves. Here they waited anxiously, weapons drawn, for the helo to arrive.

The chugging of the jet-assisted main rotors preceded the visual sighting of the chopper. It began as the telltale *put-put-put* of revolving blades, faint in the distance, distorted and echoing hollowly as it bounced and reflected off the hillsides.

In seconds the sound changed timbre and assumed the staccato, stuttering clatter of an airborne jackhammer. Then came the big, bad roar of the beast as the Mi-8 Hip-H broke out into the open and traversed the airspace directly over the hilltop. The base camp's ETA was right on the money.

Through a screening cordon of overhanging branches and leaves, the team on the hilltop watched the helo patrol with focused apprehension. The Mi-8 swept overhead on a low-altitude trajectory, so near to the terrain below that its engine noise was deafening. But the helicopter did not pass on. Instead, it circled the SAM site, as if searching for something below.

Which was precisely what it was doing. Hunting for security threats to the missile battery located in the sector. Within the cockpit and cabin of the helicopter, spotters and gun crew scanned the terrain below. They were watchful and on the alert for enemy commando forces that might be active in the area and pose a threat to the SAM sites in the missile belt.

The pilot had conducted many such terrain reconnaissance missions in the past and had gotten fairly good at them. Deftly manipulating collective and cyclic pitch controls, he worked the helo in a loose, spiraling search pattern over the entire operational sector, hovering the rotorcraft here and there so his spotters could take close looks at individual areas below.

Positioned at hatches to right and left, machine gun crews kept their eyes fixed on the patchwork of green, brown and black that unrolled beneath the belly of the steel dragonfly like a magic carpet without beginning or end.

Behind the black insect snouts of two PKM 7.62-
mm weapons, the machine gunners stood spraddle-
legged, attentively watching the ground through the
tinted lenses of their sun visors and reporting on what
they saw to the flight deck crew via helmet commo.
They too had become veterans at spotting suspicious
activity on the ground below and their keen eyes
missed nothing as the helo hovered overhead.

Sequestered within their hiding place amid the
rocks, trees and grass, well-camouflaged so as not to
present an artificial break in the natural woodland pattern surrounding them, the Cobra Force recon element watched the slow, menacing parade of the Mi-8
as it methodically circled above them.

The heavily armed transport scudded across the sky
with the cocky assurance of a schoolyard bully, its
slowness a defiance, its screaming engines and chugging rotorblades a shout of challenge to concealed
enemies to try and shoot it down.

Although the recon crew had the firepower available to them to do just that, using its weapons was
unthinkable as anything other than an option of last
resort. Downing the chopper would alert the forces
near the SAM battery and bring in ground troops
from other sectors. The Marines did as they were
trained to do in such a situation: They hunkered down
and remained watchful but calm.

Though it seemed like hours, the hovering, spiraling movement of the Hip only lasted a matter of
minutes. Then, the spotter crews satisfied that nothing
was amiss on the ground below, the helo moved off
beyond the tree line and disappeared.

Hirsh used his wrist-top keypad to inform the other Cobra Force elements in theater that the helo had gone, and then the recon element got back in position to surveil the SAM battery below.


**B**ut they had not quite fooled the helo crew. Although the spotters had not detected any overt signs of enemy activity, they had received orders to be especially vigilant against the further losses of any SAM installations.

The chopper had not departed the scene entirely. It had simply moved off to a distance of about a mile, hovering low to the ground, dropping off a reconnaissance detail of Yugo troops to conduct a thorough ground search of the terrain. Then it darted off to refuel.

Later it would return, to either offer support to troops that had flushed out enemy commandos, or to pick up the troops for another search mission somewhere else out on the perimeter.


**T**he air was brisk and cold as a dark place at the bottom of an empty well. The soul of the man was colder and emptier even than that as he stepped off the helo, ducking beneath the rotorwash as he crossed the apron of earth in a crouching, lupine run.

At last, there was that which he had prayed for— no, hoped for, since praying was as alien a practice to Yuri Batalin as that other thing most men did, the thing of the lower parts. The Spetsnaz commander had no use for either of these practices.

Once, when he had been younger, it was true they had meant something to him. But that was before Afghanistan. In Afghanistan Batalin had seen the way things truly went. He knew then that those other things of the head and the groin were mere sideshows that fools confused with the real, purposeful acts in life: simply to kill the enemy, to defeat him without mercy and to live in order to kill again. That was it. There was nothing more. All the rest was posturing nonsense, a dreamland in which fools lived who had never tasted the ultimate reality that was battle.

Batalin had been tested in the final years of the old Soviet Union's death throes. He had survived the constant bloodshed, the vicious booby traps, the relentless guerilla strikes of the enemy and the plague of Afghan heroin that had been deliberately pushed by mujahideen and CIA to Soviet servicemen to addict them. He still lived with the death cries of his fallen comrades, but he also lived with the shouts and pleas for mercy of the "Black Bottoms," the Muslim enemy whom he had fought.

He retained other mementos too. Scalps and ears, foreskins and testicles he had taken with his knife in revenge for the slaughter of his friends, revenge for the atrocities that the CIA-backed mujahideen had committed on brave men who deserved more fitting and honorable deaths.

And Batalin also retained the hunter's sense of the nearness of his prey, that scent of game in the nostrils, real or imagined, that signals the presence of the enemy somewhere close by.

As he crossed beyond the danger zone of the dishing rotorblades, beyond the buffeting winds of the propwash, Batalin now had this scent in his nostrils.

The enemy was near. His combat senses told him so, and that was enough. The rest, that which he had come here to see, would merely be confirmation of what he already well knew.

"Sir."

The soldier saluted and Batalin returned it just as crisply as it had been delivered.

"What have you to report?"

"Sir, we have discovered what almost certainly is further evidence of the landing of American commando troops at this part of the river."

"Take me to what you have found."

"Yes, sir."

The soldier turned and led the Spetsnaz commander a few hundred yards from the bank of the river, whose sluggish surface was covered with small ice floes due to the bitingly cold weather conditions. Just beyond a small rise, a group of soldiers stood guard over an excavated patch of ground, their fatigues billowing and hair blowing in the strongly gusting wind that blew off the icebound river.

At once the Spetsnaz recognized the black neoprene rubber hide of a Zodiac craft. It was a type of inflatable much used by commando forces throughout the world for riverine action and amphibious insertion into covert operation zones.

Batalin extracted a cigarette from the pack in his

pocket, lit it in one brisk motion with his windproof electric lighter and squatted down to inspect the important new find.

"This was located here?" he asked the trooper without bothering to look up.

"Yes, sir. It was found buried right here. We have only moved it a few meters from the excavation pit."

Batalin nodded and stood up.

"How was it discovered?"

"Sir, our search details had been conducting a thorough inspection of both banks of the river as we had been ordered to do," the soldier related. "Our first discovery was a watertight container of field rations about a hundred meters downriver." The soldier snapped his fingers at a subordinate and the container was brought for the Spetsnaz chief's inspection.

"United States MREs," Batalin said, noting the clearly marked insignia of the U.S. government. "You ate none of this, I hope."

"No sir," the soldier answered, concerned about precisely what his commander meant by the question.

"Good. It would spoil your digestion."

He did not smile at the remark and his subordinate remained perplexed.

"Yes sir."

Batalin contemptuously flung down the rations container.

"What else?"

"Sir, after we found the remains of these inflatables buried here, I sent a team of scouts to reconnoiter the land on this side of the river, going on the suspicion that an enemy team having debarked here would move forward from this bank."

"And you found—what?"

"Tracks, sir."

"Vehicle tracks?"

"Sorry, sir. I meant foot tracks. Tracks of marching soldiers," replied the trooper. "The tracks had been extremely well hidden; however, we have excellent trackers in our unit, men who were born in this region and know the landscape extremely well. Our trackers were able to find the telltale evidence that a commando force had landed here and had marched off in that direction."

He pointed toward the distant mountains to the northeast. The Spetsnaz gazed into the faraway line of brooding, forested hills. He inhaled deeply, then flicked his cigarette into the strong wind, which bore it toward the river and extinguished its fire within a matter of seconds.

That was where they had gone, he knew in his gut.

And where he would find them.

About sixty miles distant from where the Spetsnaz were now piling out of the low-hovering Mi-8 transport helo, another group of Yugo regulars that had debarked another Hip sometime earlier was moving silently through a forested area.

They were not special forces commandos, but they had been fighting in a dirty, bloody war for months on end and were the end-product of a winnowing process that separated the wheat from the chaff.

The winnowing was carried out by the forces of battle, and it worked with brutal efficiency. This heliborne infantry unit was a combined, distilled, concentrated extract of three companies—the rest of their comrades had been killed in action. Luck and blind chance had, of course, played their roles in the survival of this composite group, this distillation of the human residue of combat into a force as potent as grappa, but there was more to it than only that.

Undeniably there was also the fact that they possessed the unique combat skills, steel resolve, iron nerves, quick reflexes and uncompromising ruthlessness that their fallen comrades had not been able to draw upon in times of supreme danger.

For these reasons they were alive while their comrades were pushing up daisies. For these reasons the patrol was a deadly threat to the Cobra Force recon element and flanking security screen in the forest as they stealthily moved through the dark, wind-scoured woods.

# chapter *sixteen*

The three Cobra Force commandos had resumed their surveillance of the SAM site located in the mountain meadow below. They watched from concealment, awaiting orders from Saxon at Kingsnake, the remote mission support site located in the brooding, wooded hills to the west.

Saxon, bunkered in at Kingsnake's tree-pit hide site, considered the options. The recon team was equipped with SAM-busting weaponry, including SADARM top-attack manpads systems. They were now in position to use these weapons. Saxon would have preferred a bigger kill of massed batteries, but intelligence had apparently been mistaken. There were no massed batteries in the vicinity.

As Saxon weighed the decision to attack versus the

decision to withdraw, the tactical picture shifted. Events rapidly took the decision away from him.

In the darkness of the launch systems control space within the GAZ truck, almost directly beneath the four missiles that the system carried, Private Georgi Kliment sat surrounded by banks of switches, rack-mounted communications modules and other electronics panels that linked him to the skies above and to his commanding officers at remote garrisons throughout the breakaway Serbian enclave of Macedonia.

The main system that Kliment depended on during his shift as missile launch officer was the circular radar display mounted on the console directly in front of him. That display showed Kliment the echoes of the microwaves that two powerful dish antennae mounted on a mast between the missile launch canisters sitting on the GAZ beamed up into near space.

When those pulses of microwaves struck solid airborne objects the scope registered a blip. Other things besides aircraft could return radar echoes; a flock of birds, for example. While it was true that stealthier aircraft designs made it harder to get a good skin paint, the SA-10 system Kliment controlled had been outfitted with new, more powerful and more accurate radars. These had a better chance of detecting even stealthy planes.

Kliment drank tepid black coffee and massaged the lids of his strained eyes with forefinger and thumb. He was tired, drained of energy in the same way his mug was drained of coffee. He had been at his duty station for hours and was scheduled to be relieved soon. He looked forward to catching some sleep when he returned before dawn to a nearby garrison where the SAM crew was billeted.

A sudden growling sound shook away the cobwebs. Kliment recognized the shrill tones of the alarm that warned launch officers of contact with enemy aircraft. The contact was echoed on the scope before him. The radar return was not that of a fighter plane, though. Kliment's experienced eyes could tell that much at a glance.

It was something smaller, slower-moving and less stealthy than the coalition tacair assets he was familiar with tracking, possibly a drone aircraft of some sort. He knew there were many different types fielded by the NATO alliance. This made sense. Opposition forces were flying many drones in the theater, large ones and small.

Such a fish as a UAV was often considered a mere minnow and overlooked when bigger game was to be found in the air. Still, no other targets were likely to present themselves on Kliment's watch. To combat the improved SAM radar capability, the NATO air combat controllers were directing their planes to fly at higher and higher combat altitudes, making them more difficult to hit with a missile strike.

Kliment decided he would request permission to launch on this target for want of something more promising. He informed his superiors of the contact, adding that he believed it to be a fairly large and sophisticated drone, of strategic importance to the enemy. Launch permission was speedily granted.

Kliment initiated an automated launch sequence and the onboard systems took care of the rest of the process. The guidance and tracking systems on the number two SAM on the launcher were switched onto the radar's main beam and the launch sequence engaged.

Within seconds the entire multiton APC was rocked by the shock waves and blast effect of the launch as the SAM streaked skyward on an interception vector with the UAV. Kliment kept his eyes fixed on the round, green cathode ray tube display of the scope in front of him.

A black triangle representing the SAM moved rapidly across the face of the scope toward a second triangular threat icon. The two contacts soon merged and canceled out one another. Kliment was elated. He had racked up a good clean kill.

The real-time video feed from Cobra Force's dedicated Predator UAV vanished from the field display at Kingsnake and from the large, flat-panel display on the wall of the CIC on the Aegis class cruiser *Matthews*, anchored off the Adriatic coast of Albania.

The Predator had been launched from the *Matthews* to provide the commando team operating in the Macedonian SAM belt overhead coverage. Now the spy in the sky was gone.

Losses of UAVs were anticipated any time one was launched over a combat zone, so the destruction of the Predator was not the cause of any great concern. Another would be launched to replace the lost unmanned aerial vehicle, but it would be a few hours before Marine crews could get the bird airborne and en route toward its destination.

For Cobra Force, the loss of the UAV complicated the decision about taking out the SAM facility that Saxon was trying to make at the mission support site. He would have preferred to have real-time video feed to support the mission remotely. If he aborted the fire mission now, his recon teams would have to pull out of the area and vital time would be wasted.

Saxon decided to leave the go–no go decision up to Hirsh and the troops in the field. From here on, they'd have the ball.

The recon team sitting on the hill voted to take out the SAM site. They were in position and didn't feel like they needed any more backup than they had from their screening force. Hirsh wasted no more time in fucking around.

They were out here to do a job, and that meant kicking some Serb ass. His philosophy was, you were out there, you had the weapon, you used it. Period. You didn't fuck around with big-picture tactical considerations like some brass hat asshole.

The SADARM launcher could be fired from the shoulder as a line-of-sight weapon or from the ground for over-the-horizon targets. Hirsh set the weapon on automatic tracking mode, where it would itself seek the targets it was programmed to hunt down and destroy. Hirsh could still control the warhead in flight and re-vector it if necessary through the real-time video link.

He waited until the SADARM systems went through their boot-up diagnostic checks and gave him the OK to fire. Then he launched the warhead. The SADARM round's solid fuel propellent booster charge shot it vertically out of the tube and within seconds it was a half mile above the target zone, its nose pointing down and its braking parachute deployed behind it to slow its fall. Most of the nose was one big TV camera, and it was already transmitting live feed of the targets below.

Most operations in the field were anything but replays of training runs back at home base, but this SADARM strike was one of the exceptions to the rule.

Whether it was because the system was a rare, good piece of advanced weapons technology, or because Hirsh was just having himself a good day, or for whatever reason, the strike went down with text-book precision. Once the SADARM IMP warhead, nose down, went into auto-targeting mode and began to track on its descent and send back video, the kill ticked down to zero like the mainspring of a fine Swiss timepiece.

Fifteen seconds.

Framed in the crosshair reticle of Hirsh's flat-panel display, the thermal image video of the SA-10 missile battery was presented like the family jewels.

Off to one side, Hirsh could see the white ghost image of the Bimp start to move as a soldier swung

the front-mounted 30mm cannon up toward the warhead. The troops down in the valley of the shadow
of death had seen what was coming at them and were
now scrambling to do something about it before it
was too late. Mostly, hide.

Ten seconds.

It already was too late for the Serbs. Fuck them,
Hirsh thought. He wanted to see them burn. He'd
enjoy it. These guys were the last throwbacks to the
Nazi fuckers who had shoveled his own great-
grandparents into the gas chambers of Auschwitz.
Animals like them deserved to burn, and they would
real soon. Too bad for them.

Hirsh could hear the sounds of heavy weapons firing from the Bimp's cannon and machine gun and he
could see the bright flashes on thermal as the 7.62mm
rounds left the MG's barrel. Nothing the BMP fired
scored a hit, though.

The image of the target SAM launcher still remained framed in the kill box. Only it had grown
larger now to the point where part of the GAZ track
bed was lost outside the boundaries of the picture.

Suddenly the hatch popped open and a Serb ran
out, tripping over his boot heels as he broke from the
cab of the launcher and tried to run for cover.

Run, you stupid fuck, Hirsh thought. You won't
get far but you run anyway. It's good for my head to
see you run. Now the Bimp was moving off out of
the picture, still firing, but realizing the game was up
and it was every man for himself.

Five seconds.

The SAM site and the Bimp were as good as history. The white-ghost thermal image of the SAM launcher now filled the entire view frame.

The intersecting black, crosshatched lines of the target reticle framed an expanding rectangle of flickering white light. The altimeter readout at the upper left of the screen indicated that the SADARM had now dropped to its terminal approach altitude only a few score feet above the target.

Now another readout appeared signaling that the round's thruster was igniting, sending the SADARM warhead into terminal guidance mode.

Zero seconds.

The ghostly white image expanded and filled the entire screen. Then there was nothing. But the ground shook and thunder filled the air.

Hirsh crawled toward the edge of the hillside and looked down. He wasn't disappointed. The SADARM had claimed its target, in spades. The SAM launcher was engulfed in a fireball that ballooned up 30, then 40, then 50 feet into the air.

The Bimp was now on fire too, and as Hirsh watched its ammo stores suddenly cooked off in a tremendous secondary explosion that blew the entire rear section of the armored vehicle out through the back of the war wagon.

Two Yugo troopers were on fire, human torches engulfed in crackling halos of flame. One of them was sprawled on the ground, already charred and blackened, but the other trooper was still alive and running around, crazily flapping his arms. Then he too fell to earth, rolled some, then lay there while the flames burned him to a shapeless black cinder.

Hirsh slung the spent launcher on his back and got up. It was time to move out, go to ground, link up with the others. Time to disappear.

He was dirty, sweaty, muddy, cold, tired and hungry. But he was still better off than those fuckers down there.

They were just plain dead.

Cobra Force's screening squad in the forest beyond the slope had heard the explosions and had instantly understood what had happened. Kingsnake was keeping them informed every step of the way by radio.

The squads' orders were to hustle their butts to a rally point in the surrounding forest. There Hirsh's SADARM squad would link up with the team within a matter of hours. If the two squads somehow got lost or separated, they then had instructions to hump to the mission support site on their own initiative.

Suddenly the screening squad found itself coming under intense small arms fire. The Yugo fire team that had been dropped from the chopper had caught some movement up ahead in the dimness of the forest. They had not intended to engage the enemy forces until their own ranks could be reinforced, but the situation had deteriorated too quickly after the sighting. They were now committed to combat.

Hirsh, Da Noiz and C.W. were heading directly toward the position of the screening squad when they heard the sound of Kalashnikov automatic rifles in the distance. That was followed by the faster, sharper

bursts from the Commando assault weapons that Cobra Force carried.

The returning SADARM team sized up the situation immediately. Nobody needed a road map to see
what had happened. There was probably a Yugo
squad in those woods somewhere, and it was a good
bet that the helo they'd seen scouting around earlier
that day had dropped troops to have a look-see.

The three Marines from the hillside circled around,
using the sound of the sustained Kalashnikov fire as
a rough guide to determine the position of the enemy.
The Cobra Force commandos were alert to the possibility that a hostile screening force had been deployed to guard the Yugos' flanks, but none
materialized.

As they snuck up behind the enemy, it was apparent that what had happened was only a piss-fight,
pure and simple. Probably the crunchies that Hugo
dropped into the woods by helo had just stomped
around in the forest awhile and got lucky. Well, they
wouldn't stay lucky much longer.

The Marines' outflanking maneuver was crude but
it made up in effectiveness what it lacked in finesse.
The three commandos managed to get in close, crawling on their bellies for the last couple of hundred feet,
and had themselves a good reconnaissance of the enemy before opening up. The SAM-killer team had
already informed the screening squad by wireless tactical E-mail that they had outflanked the enemy detachment and were preparing to attack and crush
them.

Hunterfly's team was pinned down about 60 yards

on the opposite side of Hugo's infantry, directly on the diagonal from Hirsh's squad's position. They were down on their faces and bellies behind the cover of part of an old Roman wall—Caesar's legions had been up and down these mountains thousands of years before and there was still plenty of moss-encrusted rubble lying around—but the cover they afforded was pretty thin.

Hirsh suggested that a squad draw Hugo's fire while his crew snuck in closer. When they got up close enough, Hirsh and his team could open up with automatic weapons fire and hand grenades and settle the Yugos' hash real fast. Hirsh's squad waited until the firefight began to rage again, then signaled the other Marine element to make its moves.

It was elbows, shins and bellies for the first couple of seconds, at least until they were within grenade-pitching distance of Hugo. But now they could clearly see the squad of troops deployed in a defensive line behind the cover of rocks and trees.

Hirsh got to his feet. Chicken Wire's trusty Pig spoke before Hirsh squeezed the trigger on his Commando. The M60E3's muzzle spat out 7.62mm bullets at a rapid cycling rate, the green tracers raking across the Serb positions in a snaking, incandescent stream, almost like water from a hose. The enemy troops in the line of fire were cut down by the incredible firepower of the Pig where they stood.

While C.W. hosed down Hugo with the M60, two other Marines pulled mini-grenades from their MOLLE webbing and pitched them at the enemy troops.

Before the first two grenades hit, they were already lobbing a second set of antipersonnel munitions at the enemy. There were two loud bangs and the groans of men who were hit by blast and shrapnel, lifted off their feet and killed or wounded. Then the other pair of grenades went off, killing yet more of the enemy.

Chicken Wire's Pig was still spitting fire when the flanking squad opened up with its assault weapons, killing any Serbs that were still alive.

Cobra was following a take-no-prisoners policy. This was a recon by fire. They asked no quarter and they gave none back.

The squad moved in, guns blazing, while Hunterfly's team brought up the rear to finish the job.

The Marines counted the bodies after the firefight.

The score: 22 to 0.

The combined SAM-killer and screening elements now formed up into a single unit and hustled out of the fire zone toward their woodland rally point. The team knew that the firefight was bound to have attracted the attention of the Mi-8 helo crew, and they were not to be proven wrong.

The crew of the enemy helo that had been orbiting not far from the firefight had seen the gun flashes below and heard the din of the firefight. The chopper had then tried to break squelch at the Yugo team it had dropped but had gotten no reply on any communications channel. The chopper was now on the hunt for whatever was still alive down there, assuming that it was the enemy and not their own people.

The chopper still had a squad-strength reserve of Yugo soldiers onboard and it now STABO-dropped them into the forest, the men clustered together at various points on a single line.

These Yugo troops had orders to track the enemy in the forest but not to engage them. When they made contact with unfriendly forces they were to radio back the enemy's position.

The helo would in turn radio the nearest garrison for more troops, then sweep in and try to slam the enemy commando elements using its own weapons. Rocket fire and heavy machine guns might work where other approaches had thus far failed.

# chapter *seventeen*

The Spetsnaz chief heard the battlefield report while en route by helicopter to the mission jump-off point. A SAM site in Sector Blue had been utterly destroyed in a lightning commando assault only a short time beforehand.

The damage to the missile launcher had been total. There were no reported survivors as yet. The entire SAM battery and most of its armored security platoon had been wiped out by a powerful munitions strike.

From the specifics of the report Batalin suspected that the American commando teams had used some form of man-portable standoff missile system to inflict that kind of devastating damage. Nothing else made sense, yet all indications pointed to a top-attack missile or artillery shell, something like the European

Stryx or the American SADARM systems found in NATO arsenals.

Batalin pondered this breaking information and added it to the sum total of his knowledge base on the coming confrontation. His ground trackers, working their way eastward over rugged mountainous country from the point on the river where they had discovered signs of enemy commando inflatables, had pursued the trail of their quarry with efficiency, valor and skill. Trained dogs had been used during parts of the hunt with encouraging success.

These efforts had hit paydirt only a few hours before, when the tracker teams had found clear evidence of commando penetration of a remote sector of almost virgin forest far from human habitation. Batalin had gotten out a military map of the area and checked the vicinity against his knowledge of the terrain.

His thinking was confirmed by what his troops in the field were telling him. The area was the perfect location for a covert mission support site. Sniffing the nearness of his quarry almost with the same certainty as the dogs tracked their spoor, Batalin issued orders for the troops to proceed no further and await his instructions.

He was now on his way toward the area with a transport helo full of a platoon of his best Spetsnaz. These were men he had personally trained in the arts of commando warfare, and whom he had no doubts had what it took to engage and destroy the American commando forces hiding out in the interior.

The radio message concerning the destruction of

the SAM battery had momentarily unnerved him, because the SAM site lay many kilometers from the
sector of mountain country to which he was now has-
tening with his troops. But Batalin's next thoughts
dispelled all doubts, and indeed confirmed his earlier
suspicions concerning the nature of the opposing
forces.

Undoubtedly the SAM installation had been destroyed by a squad element hived off a larger commando force. This was encouraging, because it
promised the possibility of engaging an American
unit that was understrength and in disarray. Batalin
could hope for nothing better. He was confident that
he would smash the bastards to bits.

Suddenly a voice again broke through the squelch:
a new situation report from the battlefield coming in
over secure radio. The new report concerned engagement by friendly troops conducting a routine security
search of the forested area surrounding the SAM battery emplacement.

A telex followed: In the course of this activity the
troops had encountered an enemy formation in the
forest and engaged same in a firefight. The Yugo security detail had been wiped out, it was reported, but
a second element had been STABO-dropped into the
forest and was now in pursuit of the fleeing enemy
saboteurs. The helicopter gunship was lending air
support to the land forces while troop reinforcements
were awaited.

Batalin read the telexed dispatch and placed it in a
side pocket of his BDU trousers. This was excellent
news. Now he knew that the American force, while

having done great damage to friendly SAM capability, had nevertheless been split in half. Thus divided it would be far easier to destroy than if the force had been given a chance to form up and close ranks after the attack.

The Spetsnaz chief was encouraged. He lit a cigarette and turned to his men, webbed down onto the benches along the helo's port and starboard bulkheads. He would relay the good news to them, which would boost their morale.

To good warriors, the scent of enemy blood in the nostrils works much as an aphrodisiac does on a lover. Spring might not yet have arrived, but American blood was definitely in the air.

**H**irsh outranked the other Cobra NCOs and so he issued orders in rapid-fire sequence. The force had sustained light casualties in the firefight with Yugo troops, although none of them were more serious than lacerations from shell fragments.

Still, they were on the run and their movement was not so much an organized withdrawal as a fighting retreat. In fact, it was technically an anabasis, which was an overland retreat into mountainous country. From classical warfare to the present day, the anabasis was always a chancy proposition for those who undertook it. For some, it had meant safety and the chance to regroup, and return to fight another day, but for others it had merely forestalled inevitable destruction.

Hirsh entertained no illusions. The plan had been

to stage a covert exfiltration after a strike on the SAM site, using the confusion sown amidst the enemy ranks to help cover the team's withdrawal.

Instead, the Marines had been surprised by a platoon-strength enemy patrol just as they had begun to withdraw through the woods. The firefight had been brief, bloody and largely one-sided, with victory going to the Marines only because Hirsh's team had been able to outflank the Yugos.

The Marines had escaped, but for how long? There was still a day's march ahead of them and by this time enemy forces would have been alerted to the firefight. The Marines had to prepare for and expect the eventuality of more unfriendly troops being sent in after them, because the enemy knew there were U.S. commandos operating in the region.

On top of this, they were—at least temporarily— without UAV overhead imaging. There was still the Improved Crystal satellite photointel, but it wasn't as reliable or as fine-tunable an instrument for spotting movements of enemy infantry formations—which was their chief threat right now—as was a drone cruising only a few thousand to a hundred feet overhead.

Hirsh deployed his land forces with tripwire elements at the four compass points satelliting the troop's main body. These point forces could potentially outflank any Yugo troops that might have infiltrated the woodland area and try to stage a surprise attack on the withdrawing Marines, enabling Cobra to quickly counterattack and destroy the enemy.

This, as it turned out, was a prudent move, because

the Yugo infantry squad that the Mi-8 Hip had STABO-dropped into the forest was approaching the Marines' position and contact was imminent.

Saxon issued orders for the Kingsnake team to break camp and sanitize the mission support site. The team worked quickly to bury garbage, shovel dirt into the tree pit and erase any sign of its presence in the area as thoroughly as possible.

Saxon had allotted only a short time for this and wanted to move his people out as quickly as could be managed. It was entirely likely that enemy patrol activity would increase in all sectors of the theater and he didn't want to be caught napping.

The strategy was to make for rally point Gold, link up with Hirsh's SAM-killer team that had just taken out the mobile missile battery and was now in transit through the wooded mountain country and extract by helo.

Saxon's final action prior to leaving Kingsnake was in fact to order in an Osprey to extract the team from the rally point. In taking out a multiple SAM battery that provided coverage for an entire sector, a wide air corridor was now open to NATO tacair. And from reports the opening was being exploited to the max. The Marines had been successful. They had done their jobs and it was now time to leave.

Spetsnaz chief Batalin received a status report from his troops in the field. The scout patrols had inserted silently into the heavily forested area where the American commando formation was suspected to have been in operation for the past week, at a minimum.

He had trained his men to be human chameleons in the forest. He had shown them how to evade detection by hostile patrols and how to conceal their movements from surveillance planes and unmanned aerial vehicles, which the Americans were fond of using in conjunction with ground troops.

Batalin's training regimen was harsh but it had paid off in endowing his personnel with life-saving competence. The Spetsnaz patrols were not long in the vicinity of the Americans when one of them, Team Green, radioed back that they had established visual contact with a force of unfriendlies moving through the forest on a northeasterly line of march.

They were watching them now, from concealed positions, and had no doubt from the way they deployed themselves that they were facing well-trained commando assault forces. The Team Green commander asked permission to stage an ambush on the unfriendlies.

Batalin did not give the order, however. Nor would he do so quite yet. First he would move Team White in to bracket the commandos on their front and rear flanks. Then, once they were inside a kill sack, he would issue the order to take them down. The unfriendly force would be caught between the closing steel walls of a vice and crushed. Better to wait and do the job right than to strike prematurely and risk victory being snatched away.

\*     \*     \*

The ominous rattle of submachine guns and automatic assault rifles echoed suddenly through the dense canopy of forest vegetation.

"We're taking fire," Mooner radioed Hirsh. Mooner was hunkering down behind the cover of a rotted, fungus-covered log. "Coming from the right."

"What's the disposition of the attacking force?"

"From the concentration of fire and what we can see of their positions, I say we're dealing with something like a six-man squad."

Hirsh ordered the team element to maintain its position for the time being, returning fire but not breaking cover to stage a counterattack. Hirsh then radioed the other orbiting two-man satellite teams he'd deployed as security pickets around the main body of the platoon-strength element. He wanted to see if either of the other elements was also taking fire.

They weren't, as it turned out. This told Hirsh that the attacking Yugo troops comprised a small unit that had gotten lucky and spotted one of the satellite details in the woods. That they'd opened right up and not made an attempt to trail the Marines showed that they were green and trigger-happy.

Hirsh guessed that these guys popping caps out there in the woods were an offshoot of the original security patrol that had caught his people on extraction from the wooded fringe of the hillside after doing the SAM site. He figured that the chopper had kept some troops in reserve and that it was those reserve troops that were now using up their ammunition trying to gun down his men.

For the Yugos it would be like throwing good money after bad.

Hirsh hadn't the slightest doubt that his Marines could mop up the squad in no time flat. What he was worried about was the gunship itself—it was probably still circling around somewhere above the tree line—because it would have those big, fat doorguns and rockets. He was also worried about reinforcements that might be on the way.

Whoever had sent in those Yugo reserves had done so for only one reason: to pin down or slow down the escaping Marine commando force until a sizable contingent of troops arrived.

With real numbers on the enemy side, the Marines' cause would be lost. Hugo could saturate the forest with troops and just steamroll them. They wouldn't stand a chance. Hirsh knew their single chance was to take out the unfriendlies in the woods, evade the chopper and make tracks in a big way.

Hirsh picked a five-man action squad and sent it to outflank the Yugo position while ordering Mooner's team to stay put and telling them what had happened. When the squad was in position, Hirsh closed the trap. The Yugos didn't know what had hit them. It was just like shooting fish in a barrel.

Approached from the side, the squad simply aimed a SMAW at where the troops were deployed and pulled trigger. The 83mm rocket with its shaped charge, high explosive warhead slammed into the mass of men and blasted them all straight to kingdom come. Getting close in, out came the combat knives. The Cobra team bent and drove the steel blades into the bodies, to make certain they were all dead. They then wiped the bloody knives clean on leaves and grass.

The squad was moving out when suddenly there was the explosion of a rocket strike that shook the forest floor. Looking up, the Marines saw the ugly steel dragonfly darting and hovering right above them. The helo was firing down into their position, hammering out machine gun fire before circling around again to position itself for another rocket salvo. The surprise attack from above killed two Marines and wounded several others.

Marines were trying to hit their airborne antagonist with automatic weapons fired up through the trees. But the dodging, dancing helicopter was a difficult target to draw a bead on; its silhouette was broken up by the pattern of overhanging branches and the dazzle of the bright sun pouring down through them.

The chopper had the advantage in firepower and mobility. It maneuvered into position and, while the doorgunners poured heavy machine gun fire down into the woods to pin down the troops and prevent them from accurately sighting on the helo, the pilot launched another rocket salvo at the enemy troops.

The high explosive rounds slammed into the ground below with devastating impact and lethal concussive force. The ground shook, and the quaking earth sent up brown clods of dirt and shattered rubble. Tree branches were lopped off and the dark haze of earth and pulverized rubble obscured the vision of the

Marines. They were trapped in a burning, choking fog of death. Now they couldn't even see the helo above them. They were caught like rats in a cage.

The helo's crew sensed their predicament. Hugo knew that it was time to close in for the kill, an opportunity not to be missed.

The helo swept around in lazy circles, giving both right and left doorgunners ample opportunity to pour down thousands of rounds of automatic fire into the darkness and carnage of the woods. When the Marines had finished getting their hot shower of bullets, the pilot maneuvered the helo into position and launched another two rocket salvos, one immediately after the other, from port and starboard dispensers.

Nothing could live down there. The Mi-8 aircrew had no doubt that they had killed all of the enemy soldiers.

They were close, but not entirely correct. Mooner hunkered down in a natural cavern formed under an overhang of massive boulders. He had one of the crew's last SADARM rounds. From his protected position he launched the round and it quickly gained altitude, soaring high above the helicopter. Then he manually guided the SADARM down toward the chopper hanging below it.

SADARM was designed for far more slowly moving machinery. But the helo pilot's attention was riveted on the destruction directly below. He did not see the round coming down on them, and the helo presented a nearly stationary target to the top-attack warhead. That was all it needed. In seconds the SADARM round exploded, crashing through the

cabin roof of the Hip and almost simultaneously det-
onating.

The blast was powerful enough to blow apart a
main battle tank. It was easily powerful enough to
disintegrate the unarmored and comparatively wafer-
thin hull of a helo and ignite the highly flammable
fuel stores in its gas tanks. Only a puff of smoke
remained to indicate the place in the blue sky where
the helo had been only seconds before.

The threat from the sky was gone now. But the
attack had taken its toll on the Marine force, a heavy
toll. As the pall of smoke cleared, many dead and
wounded were left in the aftermath of battle. There
was no time to bury those killed in action. The survivors had to escape the strike zone and put distance
between them and it as soon as possible if they too
were not to be wiped out.

As Hirsh's badly mauled team was withdrawing,
Saxon's force found itself caught in the middle
of an intense firefight. The attack had materialized
suddenly and it had been expertly executed. In fact,
it had been staged by a master.

Batalin had deployed a mix of screening and diversionary forces trained in woodland operations.
Two of those forces had been fielded as diversionary
elements.

The mission of these squads was to fire and move,
move and fire; setting up a confusing pattern of attack
and withdrawal to deprive the target force of a clear
picture of the battlespace. Where the enemy was at-

tacking from, how many of the enemy there were, what kind of weaponry and the disposition of the force, were things the Spetsnaz chief intended to deprive the Americans of knowing about with any certainty.

Saxon understood that this was precisely what the opposition commander was intending. It was exactly the kind of tactic he himself would have employed in an attack on a well-trained commando unit if he were on the other side.

Here, he understood, he was dealing with professionals. The enemy would try to disorient the force, then encircle and crush it. It was a textbook strategy, and one that worked well if used correctly.

Saxon took immediate action, deploying a blocking force of Marines to draw enemy fire and provide cover for the withdrawing main body of friendly troops.

The blocking force dug in and countered the enemy's attempts at encirclement, opening an escape corridor for the rest of the team. Equipped with SMAWs, the Cobra blocking force launched high explosive strikes at the enemy formations. The SMAW hits threw off the rhythm and pace of the Spetsnaz's diversionary strikes, slowing its advance and blunting its effectiveness.

Batalin saw what was happening and quickly altered his tactics. His Spetsnaz were now to openly pursue enemy forces, to destroy them while they remained in a disarrayed stated of withdrawal.

Anticipating that his adversary would shift tactics once the Marines had escaped the trap, Saxon split up his force, hiving off two-man buddy teams to harass the enemy's flanks during pursuit and so slow it down.

Saxon's command decisions proved effective. With Cobra teams biting their fangs into the enemy's flanks as it trailed the main Marine element, the steam was taken out of the enemy's pursuit. The Marines soon outdistanced the hostile force, finding cover in the depths of the heavily wooded mountaintops.

There was a price to pay for the successful withdrawal under fire, though. Saxon had known all along that there would be. The Spetsnaz had lost the main Marine force but had killed some members of the smaller blocking and security elements that Saxon had deployed. Others had been captured alive.

Watching through binoculars from the vantage point of a distant hilltop as dawn broke, Saxon saw Marine prisoners shoved into a helicopter and flown from the distant forest landing zone. Satellite and UAV downlinks showed him where that helicopter had set them down again, some time later.

An underground installation. Heavily fortified. Impregnable to attack. His men had been thrown into a black hole. They might never again see the light of day.

# chapter *eighteen*

Vuc Dragunovic was master of all he surveyed. Not only had his Spetsnaz brought the Serb warlord the great prize of American prisoners of war, but the young lieutenant whom he had promoted to commander of a SAM battery had just invited him to view an even greater prize, one he had bagged by luck, cunning and skill.

Dragunovic couldn't believe his ears and made the new captain repeat his words.

"You have brought down *what?*"

"Sir, I believe it to be a U.S. stealth fighter aircraft," he returned matter-of-factly. "We have recovered large portions of wreckage intact, including whole sections of the fuselage and wing assemblies. I thought you would be interested in viewing the wreckage at the first opportunity."

"You may be certain that I am," replied Dragunovic. "See that no one disturbs the wreckage. I will be the first on the scene to inspect it. Is that clear?"

"Clear, sir."

Dragunovic had severed the connection and immediately ordered up heliborne transportation to the SAM site. The Hip helicopter was fueled and ready to ferry the regional commander to his destination.

It was the same helicopter that had brought the captured American commandos to Dragunovic's underground base only a matter of hours before. The helo's passenger compartment still bore the stains of blood on its floor and bulkheads.

What an extraordinary 36 hours it had been so far, the colonel reflected. The commando forces that the Americans had inserted into the SAM belt had scored yet another disastrous kill. A strategically important SA-10 battery had been obliterated by a daring covert strike.

That had been the low point. Dragunovic had heard from his superiors in Sofia, provisional headquarters of the Serb-Bulgarian-Soviet alliance. They were displeased with his security arrangements, and Dragunovic had been severely reprimanded. A high-ranking investigative officer would be arriving to make inquiries and Dragunovic had been ordered to extend him every courtesy.

Dragunovic knew by this that time was running out for him. He would have the officer from Sofia killed, of course. The death would be made to appear accidental—such as the explosion of a chopper in flight as it ferried him back to headquarters with his report.

Such measures, though extreme, often bought time, and time sometimes brought forgetfulness, quenched the fires of administrative wrath. Yet Dragunovic knew that unless he could pull some rabbits out of a hat like a stage magician his days were numbered.

That in itself was a matter of mixed importance to him. He had been laying his escape plans for some time, preparing himself for the end to the war in the Balkans. When the time came he would need to escape the war crimes tribunals that would be set up by the victorious NATO coalition, for this was inevitable.

Dragunovic had been active in Serb nationalistic uprisings for well over a decade. He had been a champion of ethnic cleansing and he had personally directed his troops to rape, murder and loot noncombatants.

NATO had already marked him down as a war criminal. If not for the unexpected coup in Russia that had installed a hardline Soviet regime and had led to a linkup with Bulgaria, which had in turn annexed Macedonia, he would have had no hiding place from the vengeance of the Western Europeans and the Americans.

But when power had suddenly changed hands in Moscow it had given Dragunovic the chance to come out of hiding and emerge into a new position of power. Macedonia had quickly become a mecca for ethnic Serbs bent on seceding from Yugoslavia and establishing a joint nation-state with their ethnic kindred in Bulgaria and the Soviet Union. Riding this tide of extremist nationalism, the colonel had quickly risen in the ranks and been given an important command by the military dictatorship that now held power in Sofia.

Recent developments had dimmed his star. The disfavor into which he had fallen due to the acts of commando saboteurs in his area of operations now threatened him with defeat. Dragunovic had been about to activate one of his escape routes. Then he had been brought the news of the capture of the American commando personnel by the Spetsnaz platoon, and the picture had drastically shifted once again.

Now it was Dragunovic who again held the whip hand. The captives were already undergoing torture and interrogation in the missile installation's subterranean prison. When Dragunovic returned from his inspection he would learn what they had told their interrogators and conduct the final questioning himself. Then he would trump the investigator from Sofia.

And then had come word of an even greater coup from the SAM battery commander.

An F-117A, shot down? Could it be?

It might.

Such a shootdown had taken place years before, near Belgrade up in the northern regions of the Yugoslavian republic. The details were murky but he had learned the truth about the shootdown. He had also learned of a Russian stealth fighter that had been shot down in Iran and retrieved by a joint U.S.–Russian effort prior to the Kremlin coup that had restored the Soviets to power.

.In both cases surface-to-air missiles had been the causes of the aircraft downings. This could very well have happened again. If so, Dragunovic would have even more than a bargaining chip with headquarters. He might well possess the master key to unlock his future. Still, it was too early to tell. He would have to curb his curiosity until he was able to directly eye-ball the remains of the shattered aircraft wreckage.

This proved every bit as important as Dragunovic had dared to believe. He realized this from the moment he set eyes on the debris field. There was no mistaking the telltale signs of the advanced F-117A fuselage. The lightweight, black, polycarbonate structural materials; the boxy, angular shape of the air intakes; the heavily shrouded engine nacelles . . . all of these plainly declared that the find was a major one.

The captain stood by Dragunovic's side. The colonel turned to him and asked about the pilot of the downed aircraft.

"Dead," he was informed.

"How?"

"Shot trying to escape, I'm afraid," replied the captain. "My men found the pilot in the act of freeing himself from the entanglements caused by his chute lines becoming snared in the branches of a tree. He had dropped to the ground when he was surprised by our troops. He drew a pistol. . . ."

The missile battery commander paused and considered how to word the rest.

"And then he was fired upon by my men. They assure me that killing the pilot was a matter of self-defense. He had been about to shoot at them, you see."

Dragunovic patted the younger man on the back.

"It's all right," he promised. "The pilot is of little consequence to us. The plane is what matters. It is worth a hundred American pilots. It contains advanced technology that our superiors will be most anxious to get their hands on. In fact, I think I can assure you a medal and a promotion for the role you've played in the shootdown."

"You are far too complimentary, sir. I was just doing my job."

"Nonsense, Stefan. Not a man in a hundred would have had the keenness of mind necessary to accomplish the feat you have managed to pull off. It is an accomplishment you must publicize and not hide.

"Make the most of it," Dragunovic went on. "It could be your ticket to promotion and the higher ranks. For my part, I will see to it that our superiors are informed of your accomplishment. I will write a report upon my return and make certain it is hand-delivered to appropriate offices in Sofia."

Dragunovic clapped the younger man on the shoulder and looked into his eyes. He could tell that despite Stefan's attempts to keep a deadpan expression, the wheels upstairs were already turning. Dreams of glory, the colonel knew, were forming behind those eyes.

Which was precisely what Dragunovic wanted.

"Thank you, sir," the captain replied. "I will continue to try to merit your faith in me."

"Good," Dragunovic told him. "But one thing

more. This windfall must be kept between the two of us. I will soon issue instructions for the wreckage to be taken away. Make no report of your own. See that your men say nothing. State that it is a security measure."

"But, sir—"

"Listen. Don't speak. And do as I say. Think about your promotion. I will endorse suitable incentives to your men to follow orders. It is imperative that this matter be maintained on a need-to-know basis. This is not merely my desire but orders from the Ministry of Intelligence in Sofia. Do you understand now?"

"Yes, sir. I am sorry for having questioned you."

"I shall overlook it. Now, you are to assemble a three-man detail to recover the parts of the wreckage I direct. The rest is to be destroyed in my presence with satchel charges. Understood?"

"Yes, sir."

"Then carry out my orders."

"Yes, sir!"

The young captain spun on his heels and was already shouting and gesturing at his troops as he walked toward the SAM launcher. Dragunovic watched him go as he extracted an American filtered cigarette and lit it using his windproof lighter.

The captain would have to be killed, of course. And possibly a few of his men. But all the dominoes would fall in due time, and in the natural course of events, the colonel was sure.

The secret of his windfall discovery would have to be obliterated for the colonel to realize his own plans. The black boxes he planned to retrieve from the stealth aircraft would bring him a king's ransom in Iran or Iraq. He could disappear and retire on the proceeds of the sale. Maybe he would even move to the United States. He had heard that Florida was a pleasant place to spend one's declining years, except, perhaps, during national elections.

Yes, Florida, the colonel thought. He might even buy a time-share condominium.

But for the captain, death—possibly a hero's death—and then the silence of the grave.

The Spetsnaz commander was back in the field. His task was not nearly completed.

In fact, it had only begun.

Some American commandos had been captured and were now in the hands of Colonel Dragunovic's brutal interrogators. The remainder of the enemy force, however, had escaped and were now still at large, somewhere in a vast wilderness covering hundreds of square miles of virgin forest.

Batalin's plan had called for surprise, speed and maneuver. These three factors were to have enabled his men to catch the commando unit off guard and to kill the majority of them. Yet it had not gone according to plan.

The commander of the opposition forces had been quick on his feet and had devised an effective set of countermeasures, speedily deploying his men and weaponry with expert skill.

Batalin's prisoners had been taken from the blocking force that had been set up on the fly to cover the main body's fighting retreat from the ambush zone. The majority of the company-strength formation had escaped. Moreover, they had done more than merely escaped—they had performed a conjurer's trick and vanished, seemingly into thin air.

Not even men who had grown up hunting and tracking in these remote mountains had been able to pick up their trail beyond a certain point. And now, the quarry had time and distance on their side. What's more, Batalin's forces were about evenly matched with the enemy's, which robbed him of the advantage of numerical superiority.

But he had no intention of involving regional infantry forces in the matter. This was his fight and his alone. It was not merely a question of pride, or even of the orders he had received from Colonel Dragunovic, his commander. It was a question of his own future.

Like the colonel, Batalin knew that the war would not last much longer. Within a matter of months it would be over and then his superiors would come looking for scapegoats.

His connection with the colonel would have branded him as a likely target for the wrath of his higher-ups, searching for lightning rods to draw the coalition's retribution away from themselves. This meant he would have to clean up his own mess. It was not impossible, by any means. Just a little harder than might otherwise have been the case.

His men were ready to proceed. The helicopter that had dropped them into the woods rose and vanished. The company of Spetsnaz was on its own, pitted against a formidable enemy. But it operated in its own element and was as well-trained as the U.S. commandos. Batalin's men would prevail, beyond a doubt. The Spetsnaz leader issued orders and the troop formations moved out, searching the hills for their quarry as night fell.

Saxon waved off the arriving convertiplane. His men would not be extracting. Not yet, anyway. Not while there were other Cobra Force personnel still in enemy hands.

Saxon thought back upon the events of the last twenty-odd hours. By any measure they had been hours of pure hell. The team had used its night vision capability to navigate the land during the hours of darkness. By now they also had the services of a new UAV overhead, providing thermal and radar imaging composites of the terrain.

Using advanced Land Warrior digital technology, Saxon was able to plot an escape route that would quickly bring the surviving members of his ambushed commando force to the remote helicopter LZ. An Osprey had already been dispatched and would RV with the team just before the break of dawn. With luck and skill Cobra personnel could be out of hostile airspace within a short time.

The Marines of Cobra Force marched through the night toward the extraction site landing zone. Saxon did not enjoy leaving even the dead behind, but a routine download of satellite imagery while the team paused along its line of march changed the picture completely.

The orbital photointelligence clearly showed three Cobra Force captives being marched from a transport helicopter toward the concealed entrance to a heavily secured underground base. Saxon made a command decision, certain that the rest of the team would support it.

He decided that the Osprey would not take them out of the combat zone. Instead it would fly them toward the installation where the Marines were now being held prisoner, and probably undergoing torture and interrogation.

Saxon didn't give much of a damn about anything in the world. Except for his men. And his honor.

Colonel Dragunovic thanked the captain and renewed his promise to write him up for a medal once he returned to base.

The precious cargo that had been salvaged from the wreckage of the American F-117A stealth fighter that had been shot down by an SA-10 surface-to-air missile had been crated up and carefully loaded onboard the helicopter. It was now securely tied down to the deck and bulkheads and ready for transport to the colonel's underground installation.

Once the cargo was secured, the colonel had given orders to the captain to destroy the unneeded sections of the wrecked Stealth's fuselage. These sections of the aircraft accounted for most of the airframe, amounting to several tons of scrap to be blasted to pieces.

By now the secrets of stealth were open to even minor-league world powers, so except for a few samples taken from the skin of the aircraft, the rest of the airframe had no technological or military value to Dragunovic.

The sophisticated electronics housed within that airframe were another matter entirely, however. They were constantly being changed, upgraded, improved, redesigned by the Americans, and no power on earth could surpass them in this.

These electronics modules, all with highly classified functions, were the so-called black boxes carried by the aircraft and were worth a king's ransom on the black market. And now Dragunovic had them in his possession.

Only a few procedural problems now stood between his holding onto them in complete security while arranging for their sale through his extensive channels on the international black market. One of these problems was about to be taken care of.

This concerned the supposedly secret policy of the U.S. government when faced with a so-called Broken Sabre condition. Broken Sabre was the code word for the disappearance or downing of a stealth aircraft. The term derived from the related code word Broken Arrow, signifying the loss of nuclear weapons.

Stealth technology was as highly valued by the Americans as were its nuclear forces, and with good reason. Stealth was an unsurpassed force multiplier. It had revolutionized warfare and given the Americans an edge over the rest of the world's military forces that none could equal.

The secret American policy in a Broken Sabre condition was to spare no effort in retrieving or destroying the classified black boxes carried onboard its stealth aircraft force. This meant that America would be preparing to send in whatever forces it might take to ensure that what Dragunovic already possessed did not fall into the hands of her enemies.

Even as the Hip helo bearing him and his cargo rose into the air and embarked on a course toward his underground installation many miles away, he knew that U.S. orbital surveillance satellites had pinpointed the crash site. Dragunovic feared the capabilities of the Americans, because they were the most formidable on earth. Therefore he had to convince the Americans that there was nothing left to recover. That the plane had disintegrated and was no more.

Dragunovic glanced at his wrist chronometer, which was set to Greenwich Mean Time (GMT). In only a matter of minutes the American spy satellite would receive ample evidence of the total loss of their stealth plane. Hopefully this would forestall further recovery efforts by the United States.

Dragunovic continued to glance at his watch as the minutes ticked down to the zero mark. He had written himself an insurance policy against the Americans before leaving his headquarters for the SAM battery.

The colonel had brought with him a pound of Semtex plastic explosive and a timer inside a circular plastic casing. The casing was magnetized to stick strongly to metal surfaces, such as those found inside and around a SAM launcher.

Prior to his departure by helicopter, the colonel had told the captain that he wished to conduct a brief inspection of the mobile launch system. The captain and his personnel stood at attention while Dragunovic looked around, examining the launch vehicle, missiles and control room from every angle.

During the course of his inspection he had managed to secretly place his explosive charge in a crevice behind one of the missile launch tubes.

When it detonated, it would do tremendous damage, igniting the fuel powering the missile's booster stage. The entire launcher—vehicle, missiles, radar and all—would go up in a blast like a small nuclear explosion. After the mushroom cloud settled, little besides a huge bomb crater would be left behind.

Dragunovic looked again at his watch as the sweep hand ticked down to the zero notch on one of the small dials on the face of the chronometer.

A heartbeat or two after it had reached this critical point, the entire helicopter was shaken by an incredibly powerful explosion. Dragunovic craned his neck to look out one of the portholes as the pilot fought to keep the craft steady against the buffeting shock waves and blast concussion.

"What the hell was that?" the colonel asked one of the doorgunners, feigning ignorance of the cause of the explosion.

"I think it's the SAM site we just left, sir," answered the crew dog. "It's been hit. Should we circle back?"

"Negative," Dragunovic replied. "We will proceed to our destination and I will file a report when we arrive."

"Yes, sir. Very good, sir."

Dragunovic sat back in his seat and ran his eyes over the crates lashed to the deck and bulkheads. The destruction of the SAM launcher had been a calculated risk. What had just happened to the SAM site would enrage his superiors. They might even sack him.

Dragunovic didn't give a shit. Let them do their worst. What was in those crates was his ticket to ride.

# chapter *nineteen*

Dragunovic faced the new arrival, a major general from Sofia named Pavko. The investigator from headquarters had the face of an apparatchik, not the demeanor of a soldier. The pallor of a denizen of offices and corridors, of a deskbound paper-pusher, was as obvious as a blinking neon sign.

The colonel quickly and accurately sized up his visitor with only a brief glance. This Pavko had the look of a staff officer, one of those time-servers who inhabit the rear echelons and who are unfit to command men in the field. Down to the pencil mustache and manicured fingernails, he was soft as shit.

So Sofia had sent this prancing circus monkey to tame the lion of the mountains, had they? What idiots. Dragunovic laughed inwardly. He was already seeing in the appearance of the major general some unanticipated good luck to add to his sudden embarrassment of riches.

Yes, he thought. It might work. All he needed to do was . . . and then . . .

Yes, indeed. It could happen.

For the present, Dragunovic set his plans to warm on one of his mental back burners and proceeded to play a game of pin the tail on the donkey with the major general. He would show his inquisitor around, answer his questions, accede to his requests—and give him the mushroom treatment.

Dragunovic would keep the major general in the dark and feed him plenty of manure, all the shit he could handle, in fact. It might even turn out to be an amusing diversion from the otherwise grim calculations and undertakings in which the colonel was presently engaged.

The first thing that Dragunovic did was introduce Major General Pavko to Captain Jagonic, whom Dragunovic identified as his executive officer in charge of operations. Jagonic was that, it was certainly true. The captain also happened to be an incurable psychotic, but a useful one to have around.

Dragunovic had never been able to understand precisely what kind of psychosis Jagonic suffered from, only that he was very sick in the head. The beauty part about Jagonic was that, outwardly, he appeared a perfectly correct and serious young staff officer, capable to a fault and upstanding as a rock.

Inwardly, Jagonic was the direct opposite. He was a pathological liar who was capable of convincing anyone about anything if they were not an expert on that particular subject. He was also a pathological killer who could stick a shiv in your heart as naturally as shaking your hand. In fact, the colonel had once seen him do both at the same time.

Dragunovic told Pavko that the captain was thoroughly in the know about every aspect of how the colonel ran his command and could answer all of his questions. Naturally, he too would always be at the major general's complete disposal, any time, day or night, during his inspection tour. Jagonic would now direct Pavko to his quarters.

The pinched look on the major general's face seemed to soften somewhat as the colonel spoke his sweet blandishments, beginning to shovel manure upon the little straw mushroom from HQ.

It looked to Dragunovic as if the staff officer might even have taken a shine to Jagonic. But that would come as no surprise. Jagonic had a winning way about him and made friends easily.

Just as easily as he killed them later on.


Saxon had received his orders. The only question he had was how to carry them out. His superiors did not seem to care much about the Marines being held captive, far from home, possibly undergoing torture, maybe even facing imminent death.

There was not a word concerning their fate in the orders that had been relayed to Saxon over the secure satellite communications link. The view from the Beltway seemed to be considerably different than the view from the front. But that's the way it always had been.

Alone, forgotten, the Marine prisoners of war would be sacrificed to operational security. The dead would not even have the dignity of being called MIAs. Their next-of-kin would receive telegrams stating that they had all been killed in a helicopter crash and that their remains had been obliterated in the explosion. That was business as usual for covert actions undertaken by Cobra Force.

The other end of the communications link was a room at the Pentagon's National Military Command Center. The orders were coming direct from the Joint Chiefs of Staff and had gone over the head of General Kullimore, Cobra Force's commander. Correction: The orders were coming down with the sanction of the JCS. In reality it was the CIA that was doing the talking, Saxon was well aware.

Half a world away, on the Virginia side of the Potomac, seated at a conference table beneath the unblinking gaze of large, flat panel display screens, a civilian in a two-piece suit spoke into a goose-neck microphone sticking out of the top of the table in front of him.

The civilian had been introduced as a Mr. James Congdon, Assistant Deputy Director of the CIA's Directorate of Science and Technology. Congdon was, in fact, with an entirely separate CIA directorate, that of Operations, which is a CIA directorate whose subsidiary departments are classified. The Directorate of Science and Technology was his cover, as was his name.

Saxon could picture the face of the spook that went with the voice. There was a certain look about them all. Especially in the eyes. A special quality in the eyes, a quality of messianic madness. Saxon did not respect the Company's men. They were not soldiers. They were manipulators. They planned, they schemed, they orchestrated. But they left the dirty work to others. Men like Saxon and the Marines of Cobra Force.

All they wanted was the retrieval or destruction of the black boxes carried by the Stealth. Two satellites had picked up the explosion of the SAM mobile launch vehicle that Dragunovic had arranged to cover his tracks. The spooks had also known about the shootdown of the F-117A, though, and they were suspicious.

Millions of dollars of computer time, photoanalysis by image interpretation experts and the deployment of covert, high-altitude surveillance aircraft, including the SR-71 Blackbird, had convinced the CIA that while the wreckage had been obliterated, the Stealth's black boxes had been removed from the crash site prior to the explosion. These, central intelligence believed, were now in the hands of Colonel Dragunovic.

"We know we may be asking you to find a needle in a haystack, but we feel that your unit is suitably positioned and uniquely equipped to handle the job." Congdon's voice had spoken the words in Saxon's ear, over the handset of the global-mobile SINC-GARS communications unit.

Congdon paused. If he'd been expecting Saxon to thank him for the faith and trust he placed in him, Congdon's expectations weren't met.

"There is a module, bearing a certain identifier," he went on after a beat.

Congdon gave Saxon the serial number of one of the black boxes from the plane. It could be most easily recognized by its alphanumeric identifier code, SV-7, he explained. Congdon further informed Saxon that it contained a highly classified stealth subsystem.

"We don't want any of America's international adversaries to gain possession of that particular module," Congdon continued. "It could compromise national security should it fall into the wrong hands. It is important that the module be returned intact. Failing that, it must be destroyed. Is this understood?"

"Affirmative. You want the black box to disappear. We'll do our best to oblige you. What if we find others?"

"Destroy any others you happen to discover," Congdon replied. "We don't want them back. But we would like to see them neutralized. The module marked SV-7 must be salvaged if at all possible, though. I must underscore that."

"You wouldn't care to tell me why that one's so important, would you, Mr. Congdon?" asked Saxon.

"That information is classified."

"I thought it might be," Saxon continued. "What about self-destruct mechanisms? I assume some or all of the modules would be equipped with them?"

"I was getting to that, Saxon," Congdon retorted. "All of the modules are equipped with explosive charges that detonate on tampering with the outer casing. If no attempt is made to remove the casing, the explosives will not be triggered."

"We'll be careful."

"I am pleased to hear it," Congdon answered with no trace of humor. "Any questions?"

Saxon had a million, but none he figured Congdon would deign to answer, except to say that the answers were classified.

"None," he said.

The transmission ended on that note, but Saxon's inner dialog wasn't finished yet. He would deal with those classified black boxes that were so damned vital to America's national security, but that mission would take second place to one Saxon considered far more important.

Saxon would get his people out if they were still alive. That came first. If there was a way to do SV-7 too, then he'd run his little errand for Mr. Congdon and the CIA. If not, Saxon figured Congdon could go piss up a rope. And if Congdon had any problems with that, he could tell it to the Marines.


The two Marine captives watched the steel door slide menacingly open. They knew what was about to happen. They had heard the sounds for the better part of an hour, echoing off the cavern walls. Thumps and crashes, groans of pain, shouts of rage and cries of defiance. They had been there themselves, victims of the big fucker with the cue-ball head who lorded it in the house of pain.

They had been tied up and hoisted by their wrists halfway to the ceiling, kicked and stomped, beaten with hardwood sticks and two-foot lengths of PVC sump-hoses, resilient as rubber but hard as iron. And throughout it all the questions kept coming at them. Endless questions. Meaningless questions. All kinds of crap they were expected to know. Troop dispositions, war plans, dates when things might happen or stop happening, bombing schedules—you named it, they were questioned about it.

Telling them you were only a mud-sucking grunt who followed orders and wasn't told jackshit didn't matter an iota. The chrome-dome fuck kept right on asking the questions, hitting you, firing more questions at you. Hitting you again, asking you even more questions.

And then, when you had passed out once or twice, you were cut down and dragged away and thrown on the floor of your cell. Maybe the next day, maybe the day after, Chrome Dome would dance with you all over again.

Yeah, the two Marines had been there, done that. They had been captives for a little more than two days but it already felt like two centuries. Corporals Watkins and Scaglia got ready to minister to their compadre as the door opened and two uniformed Yugo guards dragged him in, holding him up under the armpits. Then they pitched Sergeant Marty Yamasoto onto the floor.

"Sarge, you okay?"

"What the fuck you guys think?"

"Take it easy, man," they said as they dragged him to one of the cots in the cold, dank cell and laid him on the bare, bug-infested mattress. All of them had caught three kinds of lice by now. They could sit for hours, picking the crawling, writhing insects off their skin, heads and crotches. The bugs had gotten fat and swollen on the blood they'd sucked out of them. The prison lice were enjoying boom times.

The Marines gave Yamasoto some rancid water they'd been saving for him in the single rusty metal cup they'd been given to drink from. They had to ration the water and food because they could never be sure when the guards might come around again. Yamasoto took a sip but couldn't get any more down.

The Marines sat down again against the walls of the cell. They knew they had to do something soon or they wouldn't make it. At first they figured they might be swapped for something or somebody else. Now, though, after the pointless interrogations and beatings, they figured they were just going to be bounced off the walls until they died, and that would be it. Good-bye, Charlie. Adios and *hasta la vista*.

Neither Marine was afraid to die, but nobody wanted to die that kind of death. It was better, they decided, to try to break out of this hellhole while they still had the strength than just wait for the end.

The two corporals had been hatching a plan while Yamasoto was getting whaled on in the house of pain. When the sergeant felt a little better, they figured they'd let him in on it.


The tunnel complex had been carved out by titanic forces acting over millions of years. Rushing water, flowing lava, the explosive force of earth tremors. All had played a hand in its making. It was truly one of the world's wonders, thought Colonel Dragunovic as he surveyed the vast subterranean realm.

And it was more even than that.

It was a creation of the only truly absolute power that existed in the world. No military weapon, not even the nuclear arsenals of the West and East, could hold a candle to it. It was power that occasionally erupted with the irresistible force of a volcano, yet more often acted slowly, almost invisibly, over the course of unfathomable eons. Yet it never failed. It never faltered. It swept away anything in its path.

There was no deal you could negotiate, nothing you could do. Nature would win every time. You fucked with nature, you were history.

There was a lesson in that, and Dragunovic was a receptive student, just as he was a student of everything in life that might prove of use or of value to him. That was how he had learned of the caverns in the first place. By paying attention, by watching and listening.

The villagers in the vicinity had known about them for as long as any of them could remember, and when, seeking to purchase local food for his troops in one nearby village, the caves had come up in conversation with an old, toothless farmer, Dragunovic had asked if he could be shown this local prodigy.

The farmer's son proved an able guide to the caverns, which could be reached by cave openings in the mountains, and Dragunovic had been impressed by what he'd seen. Yes, part of him had marveled at the giant stalagmites and stalactites meeting midway between floor and ceiling, and at the ancient cave paintings on the walls left by primitive man, and at the subterranean river that flowed through deep underground channels like blood pouring into a heart.

Dragunovic was a practical man and a soldier, however. What impressed him most was the utility he saw in those caverns.

Not only did the colonel envision in this natural complex of impregnable underground bunkers a ready-made command center that could comfortably house a small army of men, but he also sensed that the tunnel system was far more extensive than anyone realized.

The boy who was his guide had penetrated far, but admitted that there were other tunnels, beyond which he had never ventured. Dragunovic knew that the mountains through which these caverns curved and zigzagged stretched beyond the borders of Macedonia, into Albania to the west, Bulgaria to the east and Greece to the south.

If Dragunovic discovered that the labyrinth extended beyond any of the borders of these countries, he would have at his disposal an unparalleled smuggling and escape route.

Since occupying the tunnels and moving in men and equipment, he had made the mapping of the tunnels his number one priority. He had entrusted this duty to his faithful Radom, who also made certain that the three surveyors who had done the work had all suffered unfortunate accidents in the course of their dangerous jobs underground and could divulge their discoveries to no one else.

Once the work was done, Dragunovic, like Columbus, had discovered a passage to a new world, for one of the spurs of the labyrinthine complex of tunnels wound its way beneath the mountains and connected with a tunnel complex in northern Greece.

It could be exited just across the Macedonia-Greece border, near the beginning of the E-75 highway that stretched due south to the Greek seaport city of Thessalonika, beyond which the blue Aegean stretched away to the shores of Turkey.

Beyond lay Istanbul, if he wished, or a little further south along the Turkish coast, the smuggler's mecca of Izmir. Beyond that, the coast of North Africa and the Middle East beckoned. Of course, the colonel could also chart a course to the south, sailing until he reached the Med, and from there enter Europe's back door via Italy.

Yes, the tunnels that Dragunovic had discovered were truly a gateway to another world. One to which he could disappear and enjoy a comfortable life under an assumed identity in any of a dozen hospitable retirement havens. And the time was fast approaching when the colonel would be exercising this option.

Things were happening quickly. Apart from the displeasure in Sofia that had prompted the arrival of Major General Pavko, Dragunovic's sources among the smugglers informed him that the Soviets were about to roll back their forces from Bulgaria.

The commissars of the Kremlin had proven their point. They had cleaned house in the Caucasus while tying up NATO in Yugoslavia and now they would let the Balkans fall into the lap of the West like a rotten fruit. Let the victor take the spoils, they could care less.

It was clear to Dragunovic that it was high time he got out.

Now, as he stood smoking one of the American filter cigarettes he enjoyed, feeling the rasp of the rich smoke drawn across the membranes of his lungs, he stared at the powerfully built giant in combat fatigues who was loading up a military transport truck.

Radom's bald head glistened with sweat as he hefted the heavy crates into the back of the vehicle, but otherwise the acromegalic showed little strain from the effort. Blindingly bright helium-arc lamps had been set up on stands, powered by portable battery packs, and the stone walls of caverns that had never before seen the light of day now reflected the harsh glare of the intense spotlights.

The crates contained the precious cargo that would make the colonel's post-war retirement plans possible. The centerpiece of the crown jewels were the black boxes. Dragunovic had already made inquiries of his clients in Iran and they were interested enough to wire a five figure advance into his Swiss bank account, assuring they got first crack at the merchandise.

"All finished," Radom said after the last crate was inside the truck.

"Good," Dragunovic answered the circus freak. "Now what about our insurance policy?"

"I do that now," replied Radom, and began pulling electronic detonator timers from the bulging pockets of his camouflage fatigue pants.

*    *    *

The Spetsnaz chief was perplexed. What had become of the American commando force? It had seemingly disappeared into the mountains, been swallowed by the hills. Batalin had search teams out combing as much square-mileage as possible, yet nothing, not the smallest trace of its presence had been turned up.

He was certain the commandos had not yet extracted. He would have known about this had it happened. His forces were too close to the withdrawing enemy not to have detected a heliborne rescue mission in progress.

Then, as he stared toward the summits of distant peaks, Batalin suddenly realized his mistake. At that moment the truth struck him with blinding clarity. Suddenly everything came into focus. The mountain had not come to Mohammed. Mohammed had come to the mountain.

The American special forces were going to hit the base, he realized. Of course. What a fool he had been to think otherwise. That would explain why the search teams had turned up nothing. The commandos were advancing, not withdrawing, moving toward him instead of away from him.

Now convinced he was on the right track, Batalin issued rapid instructions to his executive officer. All his scattered forces were to be pulled in from the field immediately. They were to assemble at the remote landing zones in the mountains where the helos had dropped them and prepare to embark once the ships arrived.

The Spetsnaz had permitted himself to be led around in circles. Now he would aim for the bull's-eye.

## chapter *twenty*

The helo pilot balked at proceeding any farther.

"I can't do it," he protested. "It's too dangerous. I must turn around now before it's too late."

The fighter jets had appeared from low on the western horizon, popping into view like specters of death only a few thousand yards before the helo reached its destination.

The sleek warplanes were F/A-18F Super Hornets that had lifted off the flight deck of the Nimitz class nuclear carrier *Eisenhower* about an hour before. They had tanked up over the Adriatic, traversed Albania, and penetrated the Macedonian heartland through the holes that Cobra Force had punched in Yugoslavian SAM coverage.

The F/A-18s were now paying back the debt that Marine aviation in this theater owed to Cobra's SAM-killing successes. The pilots had been summoned to an emergency mission briefing in the dead of night. The strike package had gone wheels-up before dawn, their objective burned into their minds.

One by one, the agile fighter planes released their bomb loads against the side of the mountain and the outlying buildings, antenna farms and other ancillary areas. The gravity bombs rained down, making the earth thunder and shake and raising up clouds of dust and rubble. The planes then swung around and returned to hurl rocket strikes at the target.

Firing up at them were triple-a installations protecting the base from airborne attack. ZSU-23-4 Shilka antiaircraft guns threw up a high-altitude flak front of flame and shrapnel. Other low-level defense assets were also activated, including 20mm cannons, rocket launchers and swivel-mounted machine guns.

Hell was raining down from the sky and shooting up at heaven. In between, the Mi-8 Hip ferrying the Spetsnaz team toward the base was caught smack between Zeus' thunder and Vulcan's forge. Small wonder the pilot wanted to turn tail and run. Any sane mind would want to do precisely that.

The Spetsnaz commander had other ideas, though. The NATO air attack was tactically counterproductive, he knew. The base was virtually impregnable to airborne attack by conventional methods. Had NATO truly desired to launch an effective strike on the installation it would have used other assets, such as cruise missiles.

Using tacair forces and dumb iron bombs for the job was like sending in Don Quixote on a mule, to tilt at the base with a wooden sword. Both measures were futile. The installation, buried deep within millions of tons of protective rock, would easily shrug off the attack, just as the British underground base at Gibraltar had withstood a Luftwaffe onslaught in World War II with little more than minor damage.

No. The coalition allies had no serious intention of destroying the base. This much was evident. There could be only one explanation for this wasteful deployment of air combat assets.

A diversion.

Yes, a diversion. Somewhere amid the chaos below, also at risk from the ferocity of the attack, the commando force that Batalin and his Spetsnaz had been tracking was preparing to insert into the underground complex.

Perhaps they were even already inside. In either case, Batalin would dare the gaping jaws of hell itself to follow them in. Prudence, even sanity, be damned.

The Spetsnaz chief drew his personal Crvena Zastava Model 70 sidearm. He pointed the 7.65mm automatic pistol at the pilot's head. The rotorcraft was suddenly buffeted by the powerful shock wave of a massive explosion off to starboard somewhere. Batalin couldn't tell whether it had been friendly or unfriendly in origin. Neither did he care.

"One final time," he growled at the pilot. "Take us in."

"No. It cannot be done. I will not risk it."

Before the pilot could touch the cyclic pitch control to swing the chopper around, the gun in Batalin's hand coughed once.

The fatal round made a small, neat entry wound in the side of the pilot's head, but brain matter, bone and blood covered the windshields to front and left, spattered most of the door and got all over the instrumentation panel.

The Spetsnaz chief swung the pistol to point at the copilot.

"You will take over."

This time he didn't get an argument.

**D**ragunovic found Captain Jagonic pleasantly conversing with the major general from Sofia. Suddenly there came the thud, crash and boom of explosions from outside the base. The cement floor shook and particles of plaster and stone rained down from the walls under the impact of the ferocious blasts.

"What the hell was that?" asked Major General Pavko, panic clearly showing on his face.

Dragunovic smiled. He did not appear in the least concerned.

"Oh, possibly the sound of judgment," he said pleasantly.

"How do you mean, colonel?" asked the staff officer from Sofia, not understanding the colonel's casual tone but feeling definitely uneasy.

"I mean what you hear is your death knell," replied Dragunovic, still smiling.

Then, to Captain Jagonic, he uttered two words: "Kill him."

Jagonic was still smiling, but a six-inch stiletto

blade had snapped open in his right hand with a
barely audible click.

Before Pavko could react, Jagonic grabbed him by
the throat with his left hand and plunged the dagger
into his heart with his right. Jagonic's eyes widened
as he sank to his knees, pumping dark red arterial
fluid out onto the floor.

"Retrieve his papers and make him vanish," Dragunovic ordered. "We depart from the prearranged
place in fifteen minutes precisely. I will not wait a
second longer. If you're not there, we leave without
you."

Jagonic nodded and went to work. Dragunovic left
his XO and hustled down the hall.

He had work to do of his own. The moment he
had been fearing, planning and waiting for had finally
arrived.

Armageddon, Ragnarok, call it what you would—
the fat lady had just sung.

The chopper nosed down, fighting vortexes of
blast and wind and concussion, making for a spot
amidst the dust, noise, chaos and explosions of battle.
The Spetsnaz had put away his gun. The copilot knew
that he had but one chance to live, and that was to
put down the Spetsnaz forces safely, then take his
chances against the enemy fighters. The odds were
not good, but his chances against Batalin were less
than zero.

Straining to see where he was going through clouds
of smoke and a pall of dirt, the pilot reduced speed

on the collective pitch control and continued to drop toward the hot LZ he'd picked out on the ground below. He was within a few hundred feet of his objective when an explosion suddenly staved in part of the cockpit windshield, covering the pilot with glass shards.

"We've been hit," the pilot shouted.

He and Batalin both had been cut by impact splinters and their faces were bleeding.

"I can see that, you idiot," Batalin shouted back. "You're almost there. Only a score more meters. Do it, damn you."

Smoke was beginning to drift acridly through the cockpit. The pilot cursed as the caustic fumes stung his eyes.

The damage was worse than merely some shattered windshield glass. Now the instrumentation gauges were dipping left and right and the helo was not responding to his controls as it should have. The pilot was losing hydraulic pressure. The stick and pedals were sluggish under his hands and feet.

Fighting the increasingly balky controls, the pilot continued the descent. Finally—he didn't know how—he managed to make it to the LZ, hovering the Mi-8 some ten feet off the ground.

"Out! All of you!" Batalin shouted at his men.

Two by two, they jumped from the exit doors, shouting war cries amid the din of the explosions, and raced toward the entrance to the base, which gaped black and open directly in front of them.

To the pilot, the Spetsnaz shouted, "You'd better

get out too. This crate has had it. You're better off taking your chances with us."

The copilot shook his head.

"Up your ass," he hollered back. "I'm taking her out of here." He turned to face the Spetsnaz, a grim look on his bloodied, badly abraded face. "Get out."

The Spetsnaz chief saluted his bravery even as he lamented the copilot's stupidity.

Batalin then jumped from the side door and began running after his comrades, who were already considerably ahead of him. Behind him, the Hip immediately gained altitude, machine gun tracers erupting from the helo at a Shilka emplacement that had swung its quad barrels around toward them. In the confusion they were about to be hit by friendly fire.

The Shilka went up in a fireball as heavy-caliber bullets penetrated the armored skin of the emplacement, showering the area with burning fuel and sending ammo cook offs pinwheeling everywhere.

Batalin heard the sick, whining sound of the helo's damaged engines as it continued to pull for altitude. Despite the personal danger, he whirled around just before reaching the mouth of the installation's main tunnel. The helo continued to rise, had reached its translation altitude about 60 feet off the ground, and swung due west.

Damn, he thought. Maybe they'll make it yet.

But they didn't.

A rocket strike from one of the FA-18s scored a direct hit on the crippled helo's right engine nacelle.

The aircraft vaporized in a fireball that forced Batalin to hit the dirt and cover his head as a cascade of burning fuel and shrapnel tumbled down around him. The Spetsnaz' BDUs caught fire and Batalin rolled around in the dirt, desperate to put out the flames.

As he did, he heard a gunshot and a strangled cry of pain. Then someone or something was on top of him. Two hands grasped him tightly beneath the armpits and dragged him roughly to his feet. It was Corporal Vladimir Zilko, the company marksman.

"You all right, sir?" he asked.

"Fine."

Batalin saw the dead soldier with the fresh wound leaking blood from a large exit hole in the back of his head. He'd been expertly drilled through the face at about three hundred yards with a single shot from an AKS-74.

That was damn nice shooting. The front of the head was smashed to bits like a Halloween pumpkin on November 1. The Spetsnaz felt a glow of pride. He had taught Corporal Zilko to do that. But he also felt gratitude toward himself. Through Zilko, he had saved his own life this day.

"This one must have thought you were the enemy," Corporal Zilko told his commander. "He was about to shoot you but I got him first."

Before Batalin could reply, a rocket strike sent up a fireball only a little distance away, gouging a fifteen foot crater in the earth in the process.

The two soldiers said nothing more as they both ran for the safety of the installation's entrance.

\*　　\*　　\*

Automatic fire rotored from Chicken Wire's trusty Pig, its high capacity box mag feeding the MG's voracious craw at a cycling rate of over 500 rounds per minute.

Two camo-fatigued Yugos wouldn't be playing cowboy anymore, not with the bright red stitches CW's Pig had just embroidered across their field jackets. The troops were literally blown off their feet in a spray of gushing blood. At close range, the Pig performed like a high-speed juice machine fed a couple of plump tomatoes.

Chicken Wire didn't waste his ammo. Controlled bursts usually worked better than sustained fire in most situations, especially when you kicked ass with the Pig when on the move instead of from a fixed emplacement where you could reliably use a belt.

Ammo bandoliers looked cool in the movies but in actual combat they were the kind of flash that could get you killed. They tended to make the M60 jam more easily and they got in your way. With the box mag the weapon was more controllable, more accurate and easier to tote around and reload.

Chicken Wire stepped over the two dead Yugos and yanked two mini-grenades clipped to his MOLLE webbing. He tossed the black metal eggs, ducked back and heard the twin explosions go *boom-boom* from inside the room, followed by pained screams of the men who'd been hit.

He then stepped inside, sweeping the room with bursts of machine gun fire to clean out the hornets' nest of unfriendlies. The clearing smoke revealed bodies everywhere.

The area was secure.

Chicken Wire held up his clenched fist and then opened it. The signal to move in. A six-man Cobra Force squad hustled in behind him, stepping over the enemy dead.

Climbing the ladder of rank was as easy as stripping Pavko of his identity papers and pinning the dead officer's insignia flashes to his BDU epaulettes and collar. Presto. Colonel Vuc Dragunovic was now Major General Bronislav Pavko.

That was the good part. The bad part was that the base was now under attack from within. It had been penetrated by American commando forces.

Dragunovic had also received reports that Batalin and his Spetsnaz cadre were inside the underground complex as well, attempting to neutralize the Americans.

That was very brave and patriotic of Batalin. Handy for Dragunovic too. While the Spetsnaz and the Americans wiped each other out, Dragunovic would be busy getting his ass out of the line of fire.

The base commander's plans and preparations included a secure corridor on foot to the GAZ trucks that had been loaded up with his booty, ready to be driven along the tunnel toward the other end, across the border in Greece. There were many miles of tunnel, some as easy to travel as a secondary road, others that took care and slow-going to get across, but Dragunovic had tested every linear foot of the escape route and he knew that it was all passable.

Plus he had mined the access tunnel to the cavern where the escape truck stood waiting and ready to go with loyal Radom standing guard. As soon as they got inside the vehicle, he would remote-detonate the charges, sealing off all pursuit from inside the base. The only way they would stop him then would be to wait him out at the opposite end of the tunnel complex. Of course, pursuers would have to know where that was, and nobody did, except for Dragunovic.

The base commander un-Velcroed the handheld radio from its belt-mount and broke squelch as he ran along the corridor with his exec right behind him.

"Radom. Report."

The big henchman placed the comms unit to his right ear. He stood beside the car in the darkness. Wearing night vision goggles, he was armed with a standard AK-47 fitted out with a high-capacity drum mag holding two hundred rounds. The full-sized rifle looked like a toothpick in his hands. Unauthorized parties would be shredded.

"Waiting, sir. All is ready."

"Good. We should be there in minutes."

Of course, thought Dragunovic, Radom didn't have the ignition keys, so there was no danger of treachery. Only the colonel could fire up the truck engines. As soon as he was inside the escape cavern, he'd thumb the clickers in his pocket and remote-on the two truck ignitions simultaneously. Then they'd climb aboard, blow the det charges and haul ass for the Greek border.

Dragunovic slapped his radio back onto its Velcro mount and kept running.

# chapter *twenty-one*

**A** shotgun blast trashed the lock on the cell door. The special ammo had been developed in the early eighties by Delta Force and been steadily improved on. Usually it only took one blast to bust any lock, sometimes two. This one gave it up in a single volley.

The cell corridor stank of cordite, blood and death. Bodies of its Yugo defenders littered the place like pieces of driftwood after a storm. The three Marines inside the cell had known help was on the way. They were hunkered down at the far wall, using the thin mattresses of the cell's cots for cover, awaiting rescue by their fellow jarheads.

Saxon, who commanded the six-man Cobra Force assault element, kicked open the shattered door and hustled inside. The imprisoned Marines were waiting, having been warned to take cover as best they could while their teammates saw to popping the cell door.

Saxon's team found the three Marines weak but able to walk. Yet that wasn't good enough. They'd need to be more alert, more mobile, than their weakened conditions permitted. Saxon nodded to the team's medic who already held the pneumatic injector in his hand. Three bursts of compressed air sent a mix of amphetamines and glucose straight into the captives' arms.

"Uncle Sam wants you to enjoy the high, 'cause it's the only one you'll get till we're out of here." Saxon had already learned about the trio's escape plan. In their condition, he knew, it had been wishful thinking.

Saxon looked them over, sizing them up as the speed and sugar began taking effect. Sure enough, they were pepping up before his eyes. Saxon tossed each of them AKS-74 weapons foraged from the enemy dead. The team was as familiar with that particular firearm and its many variants and foreign cousins as they were with U.S. government-issue rifles.

The three Marines immediately checked the weapons, ejecting and reinserting the ammo clips and flipping back the steel buttstocks to tuck them under their armpits for firing stability and directional control.

Saxon watched the freed prisoners with a graveyard grin on his battle-gaunt, beard-stippled face. The uppers had kicked in with a vengeance. That was good. He signaled the team to move out.

\*　　\*　　\*

The Spetsnaz followed a trail of corpses.

 Something had hit the place like a steamroller. Batalin figured that the corpses would lead him to wherever that steamroller happened to be.

He followed the highway of death with his troops, knowing that at the end of the line he'd find the enemy he had pursued for hundreds of miles.


Saxon and his team arrived at the commander's quarters. Inside, they found the knifed corpse of Major General Pavko. The place was scoured by Cobra personnel and they found a trap door with a ladder leading to a sub-cavern beneath the room. Saxon dispatched a team to go down into the tunnel and have a look at what it concealed or where it led.

A few hundred yards beyond the ladder, at the end of a trail of blood, they found a dying Captain Jagonic. Dragunovic's XO lay in a spreading crimson puddle. He had been shot through the stomach. The medic checked him out and shook his head.

Saxon bent low.

"You speak English?"

"Yes, a little." He coughed.

"You're going to make it," he told him. "The doctor will give you some morphine for the pain. Don't worry. You'll be okay." Saxon felt bad laying on the bullshit, but he wanted to give the guy every incentive to spill his guts before he bought it.

"Listen," Jagonic said, pulling Saxon close. "Dragunovic. You are looking for that motherfucker, yes?"

When Saxon answered that he was, Jagonic nodded and went on. "That bastard shot me and ran off. He has two trucks full of plunder at the end of the tunnel. You might still catch him. But . . ." His voice faltered. "It's mined. Watch out, if you—"

The team's doctor shook his head. The Yugo's time had run out. The medic reached down and pulled the lids over the sightlessly staring eyes.

**O**ther Cobra Force elements engaged the Spetsnaz main body as the team confronted the enemy commando force inside the belowground complex. The toll of casualties began to mount as fire was traded and bullets flew.

While firefights raged throughout the subterranean installation, Batalin reached the colonel's escape cavern with a handful of his best men. Saxon's team was already there, having secured it minutes ahead of the Spetsnaz. Yet another firefight broke out as the Americans resisted the oncoming commando force; both sides sustained losses in the first few seconds of the engagement.

Meanwhile, still a healthy distance ahead of the gunfire, Dragunovic and Radom piled into the two booty trucks and prepared to bolt for Greece on their cross-border escape run. First, one thing more needed to be done. Dragunovic gave the order.

"The charges. Now."

An 83mm SMAW rocket strike blew Radom's truck to hell before he could thumb the red push button on the black plastic box he held in his left hand to detonate the mined tunnel roof.

Radom jumped free of the stricken vehicle. His body was engulfed in flames, but he hit the deck and rolled to and fro to extinguish the blazing, crackling wreath that now encircled him.

Once the flames had been extinguished, Radom jumped to his feet in the shadows of the tunnel. His AK-47 was gone, dropped and lost in the sudden attack, but the compact Ingram M-11 machinepistol he wore strapped into a quick-draw breakaway rig above his heart was still very much with him.

He drew the bantam automatic weapon and waited stealthily in the darkness.

**D**ragunovic's truck had not been damaged in the unexpected strike. Now safe behind its wheel he highballed the vehicle through the tunnel. The demolition charges he had intended to seal off access to his escape route had not blown, but he knew the road ahead ran straight and level for at least a mile before it narrowed to a stretch that had to be driven slowly and with great care.

If the forces behind him were sluggish, or got pinned down, he might still make it to the bottleneck that lay ahead with enough lead time to seal off the passage behind him.

A few grenades, clustered together and exploded simultaneously, would probably do the trick. Although there was some risk that he might bring the tunnel roof crashing down on himself in the process,

Dragunovic saw no alternative. This one chance was all he had left to defeat pursuit.

**S**axon and a detail of Marines beat boot leather in the direction that the red devil eyes of the escaping truck's taillights pointed. Most of the Marines carried SMAW rocket launchers. Behind them, the sounds of a raging firefight echoed off the walls of the tunnel complex in a chaos of noise and fury. Men shouted, bullets whined, grenades exploded. Pandemonium ruled, and the fog of war was everywhere.

The Marine element, approximately ten strong, had dug in their heels to block a force of Spetsnaz of comparable strength that had materialized from within the tunnels to stop them. The defensive force's action was intended to cover Saxon's buddy team as it tried to halt the escaping truck.

Onboard the vehicle Saxon was fairly certain he would find the precious black boxes that Mr. Congdon had been so interested in keeping out of the wrong hands. They hadn't been found in the first truck. They might find the base commander behind the wheel too. It would probably cost multiple combat fatalities to give Mr. Congdon what he wanted, but then, the Congdons of the world always got their wish and Marines always died giving it to them.

Same bullshit, different war. That's all it ever was for the mud-eating infantry.

Although the escaping truck was doing no more than 30 mph along the treacherous tunnel, there was no way to overtake the fleeing vehicle on foot. Saxon ordered two Marines to hit the truck with SMAW strikes.

One Marine managed to get off a rocket salvo before they were cut down by a burst of submachine gun fire, coming straight out of the darkness like a bolt from hell.

The SMAW rocket strike put a crimp in the colonel's plans, though. While the salvo had fallen short, and the rocket itself didn't hit the truck, the warhead exploded close enough to the transport to blow out its rear tires with shrapnel and mangle its rear transmission linkages. The heavy vehicle skidded uncontrollably, its right fender smashing into the cavern wall.

The truck was crippled. It was trashed. Dragunovic knew he'd never make it now. Not this way.

Grabbing his AKS-74, Dragunovic slung the bull-pup over his shoulder and heaved a knapsack full of gold and valuables across his back—his emergency escape cache of war spoils. The rest he'd have to leave behind. He heard automatic fire, sporadic explosions and shouts of contention back behind him in the cavern, and suspected the invaders were pinned down by friendly forces.

He'd go the rest of the distance on foot, per his worst-case scenario backup plan. The immobilized truck now blocked much of the tunnel. The wrecked hulk would slow pursuit. If he ran for it and reached the bottleneck in the tunnel in time he could blow down the cavern roof and lock out his pursuers using massed grenades.

He might still make it.

*Maybe.*

Putting on night vision goggles, he set off into the darkness.

**S**axon flattened against a projecting knob of rock on the cavern wall, trying to reorient himself. Some fucker was out there with a subgun. He'd recognized the sound of parabellum bullets, as well as the rapid cycling of the automatic bursts, spitting out lead almost in a continuous stream of fire. A weapon that was compact and rotored extremely fast. He'd bet money on an Ingram M-11.

There was no more firing now. A lull had descended over everything. The shooter was a pro. He was waiting for signs of movement before getting off another salvo. The next time, Saxon surmised, the shooter's burst would give his position away. He wanted to make sure he hit something.

Saxon could not afford to stand pat, though. His position was extremely vulnerable. He had to break cover soon, make a run for it, whatever the risks might be. Here, this way, he was a sitting duck.

*"American!"*

The gruff voice echoed suddenly from out of the shadows.

"American, do you hear me?"

Saxon said nothing. Listened.

The silence was broken again.

"Listen, American. I wear a nightscope. I can see your position well. I could have easily killed you. I did not. I want to tell you something. There is a fortune in that truck behind us, a bigger fortune in the truck that now escapes.

"I know where it will end up. We make a deal, yes? I take from this first truck and disappear. I tell you where the other truck comes out of tunnel again. You will have plenty of time to catch it, and Dragunovic too. You know of our commander? They call him 'Dracula' behind his back."

So, Saxon thought, he was right. Their old friend Dracula was inside the escape truck and the black boxes were probably with him.

Saxon's answer was to pitch a mini-grenade and run for the cover of the rocket-immobilized truck. Gaining the driver's side door, he reached inside for the dashboard and flipped on the headlights.

Radom stumbled forward, blinded by the intensified glare of bloom-out effect, a small black weapon in his huge hands. The light-amplifying goggles made the headlights appear like twin suns. His eyes seemed to be on fire, the searing pain throbbing and stabbing into his skull. With a shout of animal rage, he aimed wild and triggered a parabellum longburst. Bullets ricocheted harmlessly off the cavern walls.

Aiming the AKS-74 from the hip, Saxon shot Radom down with a three-round autoburst. The giant pitched sideways with a grunt of pain, the M-11 still throwing impotent fire.

Saxon crossed to where Radom had fallen and looked the giant over.

He was good and dead.

Saxon felt something cold and hard prod against the base of his neck as he stood over Radom's prone body. He was about to slip the gun, pivot and counterattack, when an expertly delivered martial arts hand blow struck his wrist. The AKS-74 he'd been clutching fell clattering to the cold stone floor.

"Hello, commando," Yuri Batalin said. "We meet at last."

The muzzle of the Crvena Zastava semiautomatic pistol prodded against Saxon's temple. Batalin cautiously moved Saxon away from Radom and the truck.

"They are dead, commando," the Spetsnaz continued. "All of them, corpses. Your men. My men. For what reason have they died?"

Saxon said nothing. He stared into the flint-gray eyes of the Spetsnaz. They were pained eyes. He thought he understood why.

There was a deep sucking wound in Batalin's chest. It was evident that he didn't have much longer to live.

"You see how it is. I will soon follow my men, commando.

"And so I ask you again. Why have they died? Because our masters, in their greed, ignorance and deceit, have used them as pawns. That is why, commando. Is it not so?"

Saxon thought of Congdon, and of others.

"Yeah," he finally answered. "I guess you got that right."

Batalin nodded. "You are a better man than I

thought. You understand. We two are comrades, brothers in arms."

He faltered a moment, then went on. "Dragunovic. I spit on that motherfucker. I will lower the gun, commando. You must promise me that you will kill him if I cannot."

Saxon didn't hesitate. He had nothing to lose and everything to gain.

"Deal," he said.

Batalin dropped the gun and tossed Saxon one of the unused SMAWs. He held on to the other disposable launcher. Saxon retrieved the fallen AKS assault rifle. Both men now took the tunnel at a lope, and what they found around the bend was a gift.

Several hundred yards ahead, the truck full of booty had stopped. It was stuck like a bug on flypaper. A rockfall had closed off the roadway and there was no way that anything would get through the remaining space without a bulldozer.

Suddenly automatic fire erupted from the dark recesses of the tunnel just up ahead. The two former antagonists, both now survivors of the commando assaults, automatically ducked for cover against the walls.

"Dragunovic!" Batalin shouted, but got no answer. "Dragunovic!" he called again. "You can hear me, you shithead! Answer me."

Still there was no reply.

Saxon now had the giant Radom's night vision goggles on his head. He thought of using one of the SMAWs but held off because he first wanted to make sure that the black boxes were actually onboard the truck before he totaled the vehicle.

While the Spetsnaz spoke, Saxon slid off into the shadows, keeping the truck between himself and the direction from which the colonel's automatic fire had originated. From his new vantage point a few yards away, Saxon spotted his quarry. Dragunovic had found a hiding place in a natural recess in the cavern wall, but a portion of his body was exposed. The colonel was listening to the Spetsnaz and hadn't seen or heard Saxon steal up on him.

Sighting by night vision, Saxon aimed the AKS-74, set on burst-fire, framed the colonel's head in the center of the sights, and squeezed the trigger, scoring a bull's-eye. The three-round burst sent Dragunovic cartwheeling through the shadows. The corpse landed sprawled across the front of the nearby escape truck's hood.

Saxon helped the wounded Batalin toward the truck. As the Spetsnaz leaned against the cavern wall, conserving his waning strength, Saxon checked the crates in the truck's cargo area. Inside one of these, he found what he was after.

"Good old SV-7. We're about to make Mr. Congdon a happy man," Saxon said aloud as he checked over the module that the CIA wanted to make disappear.

"Who is that?" asked Batalin; then, seeing the black box, quickly added, "Ah, yes. I think I have known my share of these Congdons, commando."

Moving slowly with pained steps, Batalin climbed into the truck's cab and pulled closed the driver's door. Vuc Dragunovic's bloodied corpse continued to sprawl over the truck's hood, feet dangling across one end, hands and head across the other.

"Now, commando," he told Saxon. "Use the rockets. Give me a hero's funeral. Do you know how the Vikings were sent off to Valhalla? They died with their dogs at their feet."

Batalin jutted his chin at the dead man outside the cab, hanging limply over the hood.

"You will give me that, commando?"

Saxon nodded and saluted the Spetsnaz. Batalin saluted back.

Saxon walked a safe distance from the truck and unshipped one of the SMAWs. Taking cover, he crouched down, aimed the weapon and fired.

The truck went up in a tremendous explosion whose concussion in the confined space of the tunnel almost bowled Saxon over. He shrugged off the pain, fatigue and the fire alarms klaxoning in his ears. Slowly he pushed himself to his feet and walked out of the tunnel.